CAT

and

MOUSE

K. FITZPATRICK

ISBN 978-1-959182-26-9 (paperback)
ISBN 978-1-959182-27-6 (hardcover)
ISBN 978-1-959182-28-3 (digital)

KS Book Press

Printed in the United States of America

CHAPTER 1

I am running in my favorite park which is Central Park located in the fantastic state of New York. I just cannot believe what a beautiful a day it is. I am smiling to myself. I can hear the birds singing and chirping. It makes me happy. I have not been able to smile in a long time.

In the past, I do not even think that there was anything really to smile about. I worked so hard and for most of the time that it was always my peers that told me that I never smiled.

I never got to see my family and I did not get a chance to hang out with any of my friends. Not being able to smile did not suit me in the least.

Of course, I never wanted to prove anything to anyone but apparently to my co-workers, I was always competing in some contest that I did not even know about. Someone who could go the longest without smiling. Fancy that.

Too much melancholy. Moving on.

It is Sunday afternoon around 1:00pm on July 1.

I do not care what day it is. It is just a beautiful day. I am so happy. It is finally summertime! Hooray!

I am extremely excited to be outside in the fresh air to get some Vitamin D and a nice tan to get my mind off everything that has happened.

The sun is high in the sky and there are no clouds visible, just a beautiful blue sky to look at and the gorgeous sun to feel on my body while running through the park.

Where do I begin telling my story? It is too much of a blur. Too many memories. So many tears. And so much heartache that it nearly killed me.

So much has happened since I started my new job here as a lawyer at Greenland, Howler, and Harrison here in Manhattan, New York. It is located not far from Times Square.

I moved here from Massachusetts just three months ago. In my opinion, I do not think that the company pays me enough money but my bosses and some of my co-workers do tell me that my work is excellent and that I work extremely hard.

However, I feel as if they do not treat me like I am an asset to the firm like they say that they do, but it is a job and I like it. This job pays my bills and that is what matters to me right now.

It could be all BS and lies for all I know, but what I am confident about is they will not fire me. I just started three months ago, and I do a good job and I know how to do the job well.

In my opinion, I do a better job than most of the people who work here, and they have worked for the firm for a longer period of time than me and have more experience.

⌇

At the firm where I work, there is a woman named Rebecca Sparks. She is the main secretary in the front office lobby for all of us. She is funny, friendly, and very professional but she will put you in your place from time to time. I have witnessed it firsthand.

It happened during my first week at the firm and I needed Rebecca's help and Rebecca scared the FedEx guy, Roger.

I was standing on the opposite side of Rebecca's huge reception desk from where Roger was standing, and I was leaning against her desk.

I saw Roger put down his packages next to her desk and she was on the phone with an important client.

He picked up her coffee cup and started to drink it next to her at her desk by accident forgetting that he left his coffee back in his truck.

I saw Roger drinking his own coffee through the windows of the front lobby and put his coffee down on the floor in his truck next to the driver's seat. The passenger side door to his truck was wide open.

I watched Roger who was standing not far from me look around the front lobby for a few minutes. I was wondering what he was doing. Then I saw Roger pick up Rebecca's coffee cup that was on her desk next to him.

Rebecca looked up from the phone a few minutes later and glanced at Roger sideways and then did a double take. She caught him drinking her coffee.

He was bringing the coffee cup to his mouth for another sip and then she grabbed the coffee cup from him and then let Roger have it after she hung up the phone with the client of course.

I stayed away from her after that. I was even scared to go to her to ask her for some rubber bands and paper clips even though I needed them.

Rebecca did come over to find me a few days later to apologize and ever since then we have been good friends.

She is my only friend for right now at the firm. I hardly ever get the chance to talk to her let alone see her. I have not met anyone else yet who works here except for the two stupid idiots Stan Howler and Doug Harrison. Sad but true. Everyone knows me but I do not know them.

The truth be told is that no one has had any time to introduce me to everyone around the office yet. I am lucky enough to even know where the ladies' room is. I had to find it all by myself. I went into the men's restroom first because there were no signs on the doors. That is how I found the ladies' room. Unbelievable. Thank gosh there was no one in there when I opened the door.

Today is Friday and Rebecca has offered to take me out for drinks tonight after work. She finally has the time she told me when I arrived at work this morning. She promised to take me out for drinks during my first week that I started here at the firm, but she has just been so busy. That was three months ago.

Rebecca is model tall, has a slim figure, blue eyes and long blonde straight hair that flows freely. I wish I had the volume that she has in her hair. She has beautiful white teeth with a dazzling smile and wears bright red lipstick that the guys love. She also wears the nicest clothes.

She told me that she does yoga, Pilates, and kickboxing every now and then. She told me that she does so many other activities, but I lost count after the third one.

I guess that is why I am here in the park running. I want to be in great shape like she is. She is a motivator. She influences me to think straight and be focused on my goals which I sometimes have been but then I get distracted and then I totally forget what they are.

Too much information for my brain to process right now. Right. Back to the question – why am I running? Why am I not just taking in the general splendor of it all? My life. Wait. What? I have a life?

I stop running right then and I find myself by a lake surrounded by some flowers and nice bushes.

Suddenly, I stop to take deep breaths. Why can't I breathe? What's wrong with me?

I need to sit down.

No, I need to go.

I think that I am either having a panic attack or an anxiety attack. Maybe both. Would not surprise me at all. With all the stress in my life from the past up until now nothing shocks me anymore.

I take a few deep breathes and I start running again.

What am I wearing? I am wearing a short-sleeved, sky-blue running shirt and navy colored jogging pants with my long dark blonde hair which almost looks like brown hair pulled back into a ponytail. I have blue gray eyes and pale skin, but I have some color, so I am not totally pale.

My skin is soaking up the sun's rays and it feels great on my face. I have long legs, but I am not that tall. I wish that I were taller but at least I am not that short. 5 feet 2 inches.

I hope to get somewhat of a tan today. I have been indoors for months. All I do is work. I am a workaholic. I would be happy even if I got sunburn today.

I have on my favorite pair of black running shoes. I hope the company does not stop making them. They are so comfortable. I feel like I am running on air when I wear them.

I am always thinking. Was coming here to New York a mistake?

No. It was not a mistake at all. It was the right choice. So why am I having second thoughts?

I feel like someone is watching me. Why am I being so paranoid? I feel all eyes are on me but there is no one close by.

I stop running again and I am looking around the park now. There are people running like I am trying to do and then there are people playing with their dogs.

There is a bunch of people far away who are about to finish the path and leave the park.

I can see from where I am standing that there is a big open space with beautiful green grass that has just been mowed and a space where there are a lot of trees. Could there be someone hiding behind one of those trees looking at me?

CHAPTER 2

I am still standing in the park. I am still staring at the trees.

Fine. I will just go back in time since Stan Howler did not give me a choice.

Stan. Dark, tall, handsome, and of course how could I forget…dumb. Family, friends… What? Where were my family and friends? I needed them at one of the worst times of my life and they were nowhere to be found. All of them deserted me so I just got up and left Massachusetts. Should I have done that? I did not tell anyone what was happening in my life or where I was going.

Now I am out here all alone in New York. That is sort of stupid if I do say so myself. I should have told somebody.

My job… sigh.

My job back in Massachusetts was going nowhere and so was my relationship with Stan Howler.

Was Stan really going to leave his wife for me? We never had our time together, or our moment, but the emotions were truly there.

This is how it all started. We first met at the firm of Gold and Blackberry. I worked there for 5 years with Stan before he left for NYC. I swear Stan blames me for having to leave, but I must be strong and stay true to myself and say no it was not my fault. He did so many things wrong. Of course, he would not ever admit that to himself or anyone else. Idiot.

To my surprise…what a small world this is! How am I working for both Doug and Stan again? How did this happen to me? I have no idea.

Back to the story. It was my first job out of college and after passing the bar. I was so excited. Stan had been waiting to meet me ever since I had sent my résumé and cover letter to the firm. He told me that over the phone when he was calling me for the first time to set up the job interview, that he got a good feeling about my resume and my cover letter.

That is so funny. I remember now that someone named Doug had called me a day earlier and told me the exact same thing. Weird.

Stan also said that when he touched the envelope that my resume and cover letter came in that day, a good feeling had come over him when he was reading it—something about my name. Does my name mean anything? Mary Beth Strikker. Stan seemed to think so. That was all that mattered to me. My name meant something to him. Wow!

It was the day of my first job interview. I finally got to meet Stan Howler. I walked into the front lobby of Gold and Blackberry and I remember how elegant and expensive the lobby looked. The lobby was very nicely decorated with paintings on the walls and lots of flowers everywhere. There were genuinely nice sofas and small tables and chairs neatly spaced out in the lobby as well.

I was sitting at one of the small tables drinking water from the water bottle that the nice secretary named Stacy Rose had given to me upon my arrival.

I saw Stan come off the elevator. I was awestruck. I could not take my eyes off him. He was so handsome. I almost fainted at the sight of him. My eyes almost jumped out of my skull. I started to drool into my water bottle. It took me a few minutes to get myself together after that.

Is that Stan Howler? Oh my gosh. How will I able to control myself around him? He is too good looking. Oh, help me please. Mary Beth get a grip!

I placed my water bottle down onto the table in front of me and put the cap back on. I pulled a tissue out of my purse and wiped my face. I was so embarrassed. I had to reapply my lipstick again. I was blushing.

In the process of doing all of these things, I scattered my papers, notebook, and pen onto the floor and across the table. I was hoping that Stan did not see what I had just done. I am such an idiot sometimes.

I sat up straight and took a deep breath. Stan was walking straight towards me now; he was just a few feet away. He was looking right at me. I looked away from him.

I grabbed my purse, papers, notebook and pen and stacked up them up right together so that they were in a neat pile again. I tried to steady my breathing. I took a deep breathe.

I stood up from the table and turned around. Stan was literally right in my face. His eyes were so hypnotizing.

He said, "Hi, Mary Beth, is it? It is nice to finally meet you." Stan looked at me with those eyes like he was trying to find out what I was thinking. I swear his eyes had this carnal look in them and then a second later the look was gone.

Stan reached out to shake my hand. I reached out to shake his hand. His eyes were watching my facial expressions the whole time as he slowly closed his hand over mine for the first time. His grip was so strong. Chills instantly went up and down my spine. The electricity that came from his touch knocked me over and I could feel the blood in my body start to heat up. I was completely speechless and I know my mouth dropped open again at the feelings that I was having at the moment.

Stan's facial expressions did not give anything away. I looked at him and then stared into his eyes and then I felt something come over me like a spell. That was how I became a totally enraptured into Stan Howler's charm.

Blah, blah, blah. Yeah whatever. I have heard from so many people over the years tell their stories. Now it is my turn to tell my story.

I know I am not the first, but I also will not be the last. I guess that is what makes it so special. The endearing moments to say the least. For it is all just a game or so they say.

Stan Howler... is a tall, very handsome man. He is a little over 6 feet tall with black hair and brown eyes. His hair is cut short, down to the back of his neck. His hair is cut perfectly. His hygiene is impeccable. He is definitely older than me, but age is just a number. I glanced down at his hands and saw that he was wearing a wedding ring and then I looked back up at Stan. You could tell that Stan liked to take really good care of his well-being and that he also is very wealthy. He is in great shape. He has perfect white teeth. His smile was mesmerizing. I melted at the sight of him.

Stop it, Mary Beth. I need to hold it together. I was salivating to myself. I hoped he did not notice. I was sure any girl would fall for him in a heartbeat.

He was wearing brown winged tipped shoes, a navy-blue suit designed by Armani when I met him. I recognized the suit. My dad back home had one just like it.

Stan's pants were not that long, and I saw that he had on black socks. I also knew that his suit was Armani because the tag was sticking out the back of his jacket. I tried twice to tuck the tag back in when he was not looking when we were both in the elevator. The third time that I tried to tuck his tag back into his jacket was when we were walking down the hallway side by side to the conference room for the interview, but then he suddenly turned to look at me and gave me this look. The look that Stan gave to me really scared me.

Stan walked slightly ahead of me then and we did not speak to each other until we reached the conference room. When Stan opened the door for me, he grabbed my shoulders and ushered me into the conference room where I met Doug Harrison for the first time.

As I approached the table, I saw Doug sitting down looking at his cellphone while waiting for us to join him at the table.

When Stan first introduced me to Doug, he looked up at me from where he was sitting, and we made eye contact. Both of our eyes lit up at the exact same time. We shook hands and gave each other shy smiles. He had quite a strong handshake. So strong in fact that I thought that he was going to break my hand and my fingers. I was in a lot of pain after that. Thank goodness I did not give him the hand that I write with to shake. That would have been bad. I tried hard to hide my pain. The pain was so severe that I had to take two Advil a few minutes later when they both were not looking.

Doug Harrison. Let me tell you about Doug Harrison. Not as handsome as Stan of course but yes, he is attractive and younger looking than Stan. He is tall, almost as tall as Stan but not quite. He was wearing a green suit, buttoned up all the way which matched his green eyes. He has short blonde hair and impeccable hygiene. His hair is cut perfectly like Stan's but not flipped over to the side, perfectly even on both sides. Doug smelled nice too. I remember. He smelled like Calvin Klein Eternity for men. He wore brown shoes. I could not see his socks. He was not wearing winged tipped shoes. His shoes looked more like loafers. His shoes looked extremely comfortable.

Doug in my opinion was well put together just like Stan, except for some reason Stan had the slighter edge.

What was it about Stan that I liked so much?

During the interview, I kept looking at Doug who was staring at me with his mouth open with a piece of lettuce stuck between his teeth.

I cringed whenever Doug smiled at me or talked to me. Did he even know that he had a piece of lettuce stuck between his teeth? Somebody should tell him.

When the interview was over Doug walked around the table and sat down next to me and asked if he could have my phone number.

Stan walked but more like ran around the conference room table and said to Doug that he had to show me around the office and had to introduce me to a few more people before I could leave.

I was not paying any attention to either Stan or Doug at the time. I was looking at my cellphone. I got a text message from one of my good friends, Stephanie Flanders, back in Massachusetts. She wanted to let me know that she just got engaged. She also wanted to know if I could make it to the wedding and if I would be one of her bridesmaids. I was nodding my head yes, but I did not know that Doug had been talking to me. I was so happy that I looked up and smiled at Doug who was giving me a stoic look.

Apparently, Stan had said something to Doug, and they exchanged glances. Instead of Doug blaming Stan, Doug blamed me. It was a pissing contest between the two of them about me. I had no idea what happened. I did nothing wrong. I was the innocent bystander here but neither of them had seen it that way.

That moment between me and Doug had pinpointed our feud. Doug's distaste for me was clear to me from that point on.

Doug stood up from the table and walked to the conference room door. Stan followed Doug to the door and stopped him from leaving. They had started to argue with each other, but I could not hear what they were saying. Doug kept pointing to me and Stan kept shaking his head. They both had to be talking about me I figured.

I was still sitting down at the conference room table. I put my cellphone into my purse. I put my purse on my shoulder and then I grabbed my coat. Then, I pushed the chair away from the table and stood behind the chair and pushed the chair back to the table.

I was walking to the conference room door and I saw Doug standing alone. He was waiting for me with the door wide open. His face was completely emotionless.

I smiled at him. I was about to walk through the door, but then suddenly Doug let go of the door. Doug walked right out in front of me and then right through the door and then he closed the door right it in my face.

I hit my face on the door. Man, that hurt.

I did not remember that until now. Now it makes sense about the way Doug has treated me for all of these years.

I had said goodbye to Stan and to Doug at the elevator. I think in my opinion that the interview went well. I looked at Doug and he gave me a smile which was odd from what had just happened back at the conference room doorway.

I looked at Stan who was looking at me funny. It made me feel nervous and uncomfortable. I shook both their hands again and said thank you to the both of them but individually.

I turned around and I walked away from them. I was almost to the front door of the building. I heard Stan call my name and I stopped instantly at the sound of his voice. I could feel the hair on the back of my neck stand up. I turned around to face Stan but I was not prepared for what would happen next in my life.

Stan said, "Mary Beth, congratulations you got the job. Doug and I both agree. I think that you will be a great asset to the firm. I mean, Doug and I both think that you will be a great asset to the firm. You will be a tremendous help." Stan's voice changed dramatically as he said this. Shivers went up and down my spine.

I saw Stan's fingers move to my white blouse that was underneath my suit and started buttoning my top button right at my neck. There was a warning feeling going on inside my gut. Just then, I looked over at the elevator and saw that Doug was still standing there with this puzzled look on his face. It made me feel uncomfortable. The whole situation made me want to cringe and hide from plain sight. Stan had been watching me the whole time.

Before I could say or do anything, Stan spoke again. "What do you say Mary Beth?" In a voice that was so mischievous.

Regardless of listening to my gut feelings, I looked into Stan's eyes and I had said yes right away without even thinking about it. I was totally hypnotized.

I became obsessed with Stan. Stan was all that I could think of. I remember looking back over at Doug and he was still standing by the elevator. He looked upset.

I remember that Stan had sold me the job that day in the lobby when I had just thought about Stan and what he wanted.

Stan had forgotten that he was married with kids and then it was just the two of us. The two of us in our own little world. We were in a marriage even though we were not even married. I did not think about me or what I wanted. I did not even interview for any other job, and I had several offerings on the table. My answering machine had been full of messages.

But wow! Stan Howler had taken my breath away. We instantly became best friends at work and outside of work. We soon finished each other's sentences and told the same jokes. We smiled, laughed and joked all the time. We spent every minute together at the office and outside the office. We were like glue. We knew the same people; it turned out that Stan had gone to the same college that I had graduated from— Boston University. Small world.

I thought that I was hallucinating. It was too good to be true, right? Well, that was what Stan had me believing the whole time.

I just cannot believe how close I had been to freedom that day. I was almost to the front door. Why didn't I just walk out the door? I had no idea what I was getting myself into. It was amazing. How could I have been so stupid? I was in love. That is how.

That is what it was. So, the sad story tells itself. I fell in love with Stan, and it complicated our work relationship after a while and then eventually our friendship.

It was only one night. I let my guard down. I should not have slept with Stan, but I really liked him. I was in love with him. I thought he really liked me too. It was a huge mistake. Love. Love was the reason that I made a mistake.

After our one night of bliss, my work was just not good enough anymore after that. My work was terrible. The mistakes just piled up right and left. It was just up to me to deal with my misery.

Stan's behavior had changed towards me unfortunately. He treated me so harshly. He did not treat me like a friend anymore. There was no more respect or courtesy anymore. He would not go to lunch with me. He would avoid me and not talk to me. If he did, he would just yell at me.

I could not concentrate. I could not focus. I missed meetings. I missed court dates. I missed calling clients back. I lost the company several good paying clients. I did the wrong things and said the wrong things.

I could not keep anyone at work happy anymore. Everything just kept getting worse and worse until the situation got so out of control that my co-workers would just yell at me all day until I left the office every night. I could not do anything right no matter how hard I tried. Stan had turned everyone against me, and I had no say in the matter. Nobody would listen to me.

I decided to go into Stan's office shortly after everyone had turned against me because of Stan. I wanted to tell Stan everything that I was feeling because I had had enough of his unprofessional attitude towards me.

I walked into Stan's office. Stan was sitting at his desk. He was looking down at some papers in his hands. I did not care. I walked right up to him and I told Stan that betraying me, the games that he was playing with me, and his untrue feelings for me were affecting my judgment work wise. I even remember telling him that my health and well-being led me to go to the hospital and seek professional help several times.

Of course, at the time I wanted to believe that Stan cared for me, but I knew deep down inside Stan's feelings towards me had been all a lie. I was beyond devastated.

There were no words to encapsulate my emotions. There was no one at the time that I could ask to help me get through something like this. I was ashamed and embarrassed. I hated myself for what I let happen between me and Stan.

Our relationship—or whatever you want to call it—was making me sick. I became so sick of Stan.

After I told Stan how I felt about our given situation, he started to bring his wife into work more times than he did before and parade her around the office and make me watch.

My office faced his office from down the hall, and he always left his office door wide open. It did not help that there were clear glass windows and doors throughout the whole company so I could not hide from him.

Unfortunately, Stan would not allow me to close my door. He would come over to my office and open the door and yell at me every time that I closed my office door. He always had to know what I was doing. Total control freak. Always want but you cannot have. That sort of thing. It made me dislike him even more than I had already.

Stan would make me watch him holding his wife's hand. He would get close to her and whisper little nothings into her ear and give me a look while he was talking to her in her ear. He would also touch her and put his arms around her. It made me sick to see them happy together. Was this a sick joke? What was he thinking? Is his brain working?

If he was putting on a show for me and if he was not happy with his wife, why didn't he just leave her? Why didn't he just divorce her? What did she have on him? What reasons did he have to stay with her for all of these years? I never found out why and I figure that I never will.

This I believe is one of the many reasons why I drive myself crazy about Stan. Why won't Stan just leave his wife? I ask myself that question every day.

The next week the tension between me and Stan grew worse. Stan and I continued to bicker and fight until our bosses pulled us both into one of the many conference rooms and said to us that one of us had to leave because it was causing too many problems within the firm.

Stan decided that he would leave the firm two months later. We did not see each other at all. We avoided each other at all costs. We did not speak to each other until his last day at the firm. He came into my office without knocking. He approached my desk as I was typing. He stood right in front of my desk. I stopped typing and looked up at him.

Stan said to me, "You will not be as good as me Mary Beth. You can try your hardest, but you will not succeed. I built this firm up to what it is now. You will not be able to take that away from me ever. My name will always echo these hallways long after I am gone. Try to do that on your own."

Oh, here he is. On his last day. Figures that he would say something like this to me. He has to have the last word. Alright. Ok Stan. What do I say to someone like you?

I looked away from Stan and put my head down towards my keyboard and shook my head for about a minute. Then I picked my head up and looked Stan right in his eyes and I said, "Whatever you want to tell yourself Stan is fine with me. Goodbye." And with that he looked at me for a long time and then he turned and walked out the door.

I did not want to give Stan the satisfaction, but I did cry in my office for a while after he had left. Doug? Is that Doug? I swear it was Doug, but I did not get a good look. I saw his face for only a second. I wonder why he came to see me. What a shock!

I stood up and walked over to my office doorway and looked around, but no one was there. I went back to sit at my desk. I was in misery for the rest of the day. I could not focus. I just cried at my desk until it was time to leave. When I went home that night, I cried myself to sleep.

The very next morning I decided to stay on at the firm of Gold and Blackberry. I did not want to leave before I had updated up my resume and applied for other jobs.

Before I left the firm of Gold and Blackberry, I wanted to prove to myself and to my co-workers that I was a good lawyer and not what Stan had painted me as. I stayed at Gold and Blackberry for one more year after Stan had left for New York before I eventually left the firm on my own.

It turned out alright in the end when I was leaving the firm of Gold and Blackberry. My co-workers and my bosses had told me so. They were sad to see me go. Everyone had said that I had become a great lawyer and that they were all so proud of me.

I headed to New York because as I was applying to jobs in different states, New York was where the best jobs seemed to be. I was not thinking at the time that one of these firms would be where Stan and Doug would be working at. I was thinking that I would not ever have to see them again. Chapter closed.

I came back to reality then. Wow! What a nightmare that was. My flash backs come and go sometimes, but I would rather forget that any of it had ever happened.

Anyway. I need to get going. I need to get home. I left the park and headed back to my car. On my way back to my car, I still had that creepy feeling that someone was watching me.

CHAPTER 3

You have got to be kidding me! New York is such a big place and of all the jobs in New York I have to come to a firm where the people interviewing me happen to be none other than Stan Howler and Doug Harrison! How did this happen? What are the chances? I was so shocked and disgusted when I found out in the lobby. I had no idea. I am so angry right now.

Stan told me during my interview that he felt bad about what had happened back in Massachusetts and that he wanted to help me to get the interview with the firm when my resume was put onto his desk.

Stan also informed me that Doug was happy that I was interviewing for the open position at the firm as well, but I did not believe him for a second.

Stan and Doug were still up to their old tricks I just knew it. It actually took me about a month to figure it out, but by then I could not leave because I had already bought a house because Stan convinced me to.

I thought that things would be different this time around, but it turned out to be the exact same as it was back in Massachusetts. Stan and Doug make themselves look good by making me look bad. It just never ends.

I had a horrible review about my performance on Monday morning, just two months after I had just started at this new firm, Greenland, Howler, and Harrison.

So much for the all the praise and glory that I had given to myself. Stupid Mary Beth.

I thought that I was doing a great job at this new place of business, but I thought wrong. After my awful review, on Monday, Stan did not speak to me at all. Not even a glance or a wave. He completely ignored me like I did not even exist.

Sounds so familiar.

On Thursday morning of the same week however, Stan suddenly walked straight right into my office without knocking and scared me. He dropped so many boxes everywhere in my office that my office was not even visible anymore.

How would I escape?

Stan was clearly out of breath. He sat down in one of my office chairs in front of my desk. Stan started to talk to me, and he sounded like he was so disappointed in me.

"Mary Beth. How do I put this nicely? That despite your review here at the office on Monday morning you must review and fix every mistake on every single one of these client files. I want you to work on them and fix them as soon as possible. Even if it means staying all night, then you are going to have to stay here the entire night. I hope you brought your sleeping bag and a pillow."

My mouth dropped open, and I tried to speak, but Stan got out of the chair so fast and came around my desk. He came close enough to my face that I could feel his breath on my cheek, and he put his finger up to my lips to stop me from speaking.

Stan looked me straight in the eye when he spoke to me. "End of story Mary Beth. Not a word and close your mouth shut. I do not wish to hear any excuses on your part. You have done enough crap work here don't you think?" Stan pointed to the boxes in my office.

Stan removed his finger from my lips and took a few steps back. He looked around my office with a sneer on his face, kicked a box on the floor that was in his way and then stormed out of my office.

I can hear Stan muttering words underneath his breath down the hall, but I cannot understand them. He is incredibly angry at me. I watch him walk into Doug's office and heard him slam the door shut.

I am still sitting at my desk completely frozen. I am totally shocked. A half an hour later I saw Stan come out of Doug's office and then go into his office and slam his door shut. Shortly after Stan's secretary, Maggie Marigold knocked on his door with lots of papers for him sign. Stan opened the door and came out into the hallway; he took the papers from her hands and then just threw them up in the air and looked at her and then went back into his office and slammed the door shut again. Maggie picked up the papers and then went back to her desk.

I stand up from my desk because I want to go over and help Maggie pick of the papers, but I am afraid to leave my office.

I stop looking over at Stan's office. I focus my attention to my office. I slowly look around my office to see all the boxes. I know that I have put so much hard work into every single one of them and now I have several mistakes in them. This is not possible. I am angry. I walk over to my office door and close it. I also turn out the lights to my office. I do not care.

How could all these boxes be mine?

Crap as Stan so nicely put it.

How is this possible? I am a good lawyer.

Stan, I swear is doing this on purpose so I will not succeed. He does this so I will not be able to go to court and prove to this firm that I am an asset.

Oh gosh. My knees give out and I fall to the floor. I am laying on the floor looking at a small piece of my dark blue carpet that has not been taken up by the boxes. I notice pieces of dust on the carpet too. I start to feel tears well up inside of me and I try to keep them from running down my cheeks, but I cannot help it.

I know I have been doing a bad job, but it cannot be true that all of these boxes are mine. There are so many boxes! I stop crying and wipe away my tears.

How dare you, Stan!

I should have yelled at Stan, but I did not. I feel like a freight train has hit me.

I feel so dumbstruck lying on the floor. I am too upset to fight with him. I do not want Stan to see me cry. Not here. Not now. Maybe when I leave the office tonight and get into my bed then I will cry myself to sleep.

About an hour later, I am still lying on the floor. Suddenly, I hear voices from the hallway outside my office door. I struggle to get up from the floor. I turn my office lights back on and open my office door. I make it back to my desk before they came into my office.

I look up from my desk and saw the both of them in my doorway.

"Boy, all this will keep her busy don't you think," Stan said to Doug. Stan was pointing at me and the boxes, but Doug was not paying any attention. Doug was looking down the hallway and then looked down at his cellphone.

Stan is joking with me. I do not find it funny at all, but he sure does.

Sigh.

I am looking at Stan and I give him my best smile. In my head I am thinking, oh well. I can cry about it later. Too much work for me to do now. Stan and Doug are such a★★holes. I cannot wait to finish my work and go home, have a nice hot bath and a glass of wine.

Doug finally looks up from his cellphone and replies, "Come on Stan. Let's get out of here. I will buy you a beer. Poor Mary Beth must fix her own mistakes. Now ask yourself this Mary Beth, are you really a good lawyer?" Doug chuckled cruelly. Doug looks at me and gives me a nasty look. "Make sure that you cross your T's and dot your I's this time around Mary Beth?" said Doug with a sneer before he turned and left my office with Stan.

Doug Harrison hates my guts. So much for Doug being so happy that I am working here with him again. He must be wearing his underwear too tight, and it is cutting off the circulation to his brain. What a moron.

Why should I have to put up with this?

I can hear them both laughing as they walk away from my office. I can still hear them both laughing as they are walking out the front door to freedom. I seriously feel that I am in prison here and I will be for an awfully long time. It makes me sick to my stomach. Unbelievable. This is so ridiculous.

From what I can remember, back at the firm in Massachusetts, Stan and Doug have been best friends for years. Stan had been working for the firm Gold and Blackberry for two years before Doug showed up. They were working in different departments at first when Doug started. Doug started out as a divorce attorney and Stan was working in litigation. They both were praised, worked long hours, brought in high paying clients and billed a lot of billable hours. As years passed by, they both started to feud about who was the better lawyer and who should make partner first.

Stan stated that he had been at the firm longer, about five years, and had more experience than Doug who had only been there for about 3 years. Doug said that he had the better clientele which made more money for the firm. They fought against each other for over a year until one day they realized that they were better at helping each other than to be rivals.

Stan found out first that Doug had a serious drinking problem and Doug found out shortly afterwards that Stan had a serious gambling problem.

They both had to come to terms that they both had problems that could be bad for both of their careers if they told on one another.

They both started to stick up for each other at meetings and cover for each other instead of fighting with each other. They both decided to hang out after work one night a week later. Apparently, they became best friends that very same night and from that point on they let nothing, or no one break them apart.

Then I came in. I came into the firm when they had just started to negotiate who should become partner first. Stan as always had a way with words. If Stan got to hire me and I worked for him and I did really well then Stan got to become partner shortly afterwards. That was the deal. I was the bargaining chip. I was the pawn.

Stan eventually made partner in the firm because I did a really good job and because Doug gave up on trying to persuade me to come and work with him instead.

I think Doug regretted his decision in the end. Doug should have fought harder for me. Doug could have been made partner and maybe have done a better job than Stan, but the firm said no, they wanted someone else for the job. The firm felt that Doug was not hungry enough for the job since he let Stan take it instead.

Stan's last name never made it up on the wall or on the company letterhead because he left for New York too soon before the changes could be made.

Stan called Doug three weeks later to be exact and asked him to come to New York with him to be a partner in his new firm. I never knew the name of the firm until now.

I think that Doug was happy at first coming to work with Stan, but now he is not so happy because Stan now makes all of the rules and gets all of the credit leaving Doug out in the cold. Doug does all of the hard work. Doug is treated more like a lap dog and a messenger boy than a partner if you ask me.

Gee, working for Stan how could you not be happy? Stan is such a good friend to Doug. I am being sarcastic when I say this to myself. Doug is so oblivious.

Enough of the past. I stand up from my desk a few minutes later and I look around my office. How in the world can they leave so early? It is just not fair! It is only 3:00pm!

"Oh my gosh," I said out loud to myself. "I am never going to be able to leave this place. I might as well sleep here tonight. I have a court appearance early tomorrow morning. How am I going to fix all of these mistakes and then organize all of these papers into the correct folders and boxes?"

I did not even pay any attention to when Stan was bringing the boxes into my office. I think that there has been a huge mistake, but I cannot argue with Stan. I have to stay here at this job and put up with their crap because I have no place else to go.

I can see all the boxes for the first time. Boxes are piled up high up against the walls in my office. There are papers everywhere. My office is a mess.

I thought that Stan and Doug both had left the building, but then Stan suddenly stopped by my office and I could hear him chuckling. I am still standing at my desk. I put my head into my hands. I am so tired.

I quickly look up and see Stan smile. I have fallen for that smile so many times. He gives me a wink.

"Cheetah speed Mary Beth, ok?" Then he turned around and walked away.

I close my eyes. My stomach turns just thinking as if Stan has me hypnotized all over again. I almost go back in time to those moments, like I am reliving the old days. It scares the crap out of me. I am breathless.

My body seems to react to his every move. I try to stop allowing him to control me, but it is exceedingly difficult. My emotions at this time have weakened and I am suddenly very vulnerable. Stan is pulling me back in again.

Stan's kisses as I remember were like a volcanic eruption to my body. And now he—and all of his kisses—make me feel sick. I feel like vomiting all over my desk. I feel the acid from my stomach coming up my throat. I have to clean up his mess. Like usual, like always, Stan never changed.

CHAPTER 4

I look at the clock and it reads 9:00pm. I am sitting in my chair at my desk, and I am thinking about Monday morning. I keep replaying over and over in my head how awful my bosses made me feel at my review from that morning.

Stan and Doug both get to go out on the town and have fun and spend whatever amount of money they want to on good food and get to drink so much wine or whatever and I have barely enough money to pay for my mortgage let alone food.

It sucks. It really sucks. I want to break something of Stan's. I am so pissed off. I stand up from my chair and move away from my desk and walk down the hallway into his office, but it is locked. I am too upset not to try again. Then the door opens, and I turn on the lights. I look around his office for something sentimental. Something that is mine but his too. Something that reminds him of me.

I pick up a photograph that is framed from one of the first parties that I attended back in Massachusetts. It was such a good time back then and such a good memory. I also pick up an award that he had earned when he made partner at the firm in Massachusetts right before he left. I get myself ready to smash both items to smithereens against the wall, but I am too tired to do it and I want to so badly.

I put both of the items back where I found them, and I walk to the door and turn around. I look around Stan's office for a minute or two and then I turn off the light and close the door and walk back to my office. As I walk back to my office, underneath my breath I said, "You are not worth it Stan. Instead, I should be breaking stuff in your office Doug. You creep."

After what seemed like an eternity on working on the last 5 boxes of files, I stand up, and then I fall back down into my chair immediately.

"*Whores,*" I said out loud to myself. I only wish at the time that Stan and Doug were in my office so I can say that to their faces.

I am too tired to think anymore so I close my eyes. I put my head down into my hands and lower my hands and head onto my desk. I dream about what happened that Monday morning at my monthly review. I think about how awful my bosses and co-workers had made me feel. It was awful. I cried myself to sleep Monday night and then on Tuesday and Wednesday night I could not sleep at all. I think of the things that they said about me and to my face at the meeting. I replay them over and over again in my head like it was yesterday.

"Can she do the work? She was not stressed out before. Does she need to be trained again?" said Bob Tucker, a senior partner.

"Does she even know how to type? I mean look at this. Does she even know how to spell?" said Doug Harrison. He looked right at me when he said those words. He was so angry at me.

Stan had just sat that there and said nothing in my defense. He was going to but then he closed his mouth. He raked one of his hands through his hair. He put his head into his hands and then lowered his hands and his head to the table. He had just given up on me. Unbelievable.

"What is she doing here? She should be fired. There have been too many mistakes. A lot of our clients have called to complain about her. This should not have been tolerated. What does she want a medal for all of her mistakes?" said the boss of the firm, Mr. Mark Greenland, with his head that was lowered down to the table like usual. He cannot look anyone in the eye when he had something to say or to your face for that matter.

What? What is he talking about?

Mr. Mark Greenland had been looking at some of my reports during the meeting. He threw the papers around and flailed his arms and hands and said mean things out loud about me so that everyone in the room could hear. (Idiot, moron, worthless, not worthwhile, etc.)

After everyone in the room had said their piece, Mr. Mark Greenland usually said his piece. His word was always the last word. Of course, that is what Mr. Mark Greenland always wanted to believe, but that was not always the case. After Mr. Mark Greenland gave "his speech" as he put it, he would raise his hands up and would made a cut signal with both his hands in midair.

Even after Mr. Mark Greenland had the final say, all the voices in the room at the table did not want to stop beating me up. Enough was not enough for them.

I had to keep hearing negative remarks from every person in the room until they had their fill of insulting me and shouting at me.

"Does she even know how to write a brief? Does she even know what a brief is?" said Bill Goodale, a senior partner who was totally disgusted with me.

Well, truth be told I have been disgusted with Bill the whole entire time that I have been working here at this firm. You disgust me as well. Take that Bill.

"Does she even know how to write a deposition?" She is costing the firm so much money, said Harry Greenland, Mr. Mark Greenland's son.

"Where did she go to law school?" said Kevin Hawks. "Did she even pass the bar?" said Ben Fitzgerald.

"Did she even go to law school? Someone should check her credentials, so we do not get sued," said Zachary Rowing, who slammed down one of my many reports onto the table extremely close to where I was sitting.

I remember watching Stan and how he had just sat there and said nothing in my defense. I watched how Stan reacted the whole time. That part had absolutely devastated me and infuriated me at the same time to the point where I could never trust him again. He betrayed me. End of story.

I was still in shock and in my own little world when he came into my office on Thursday afternoon of the same week. What I had come to find out was that everyone except Stan wanted to fire me. He had convinced them all to keep me on so that he could have some fun with me—make me pay him back for how hard he had to fight to keep me here at the firm.

He told me he liked my work and the way that I walked and how I looked in a suit—stuff like that. Stan thought I looked cute and that I kept him entertained.

Stan said that I was smart and that I could do the job better with his help. The partners had scoffed at what he had said. They were furious. Stan said that I would make up for the problems that I had caused.

I did however do something right in the midst of all of the commotion. I had brought in new clients. "Well-paying clients" as Mr. Mark Greenland had told me the day that all five new clients signed on to be a part of the firm a month after I started working at the firm.

Stan kept telling me how they all smirked and laughed at the thought of how Stan would have me over his desk late at night for making so many mistakes on so many briefs and depositions. They also said some awful man jokes about me as well.

Stan told me other awful things of what went on in the conference room after I had left. I remember thinking at the time how it all had me want to throw up into my waste basket. Stan liked seeing me squirm in my chair. He enjoyed torturing me. He loved every second of it. Ten to one he slept very well every night knowing that I could not sleep at all.

I remember leaving the firm at 11:30pm Thursday night and getting into my car to drive home but when I woke up Friday morning I was in the hospital.

What happened to me?

When I got home Saturday afternoon, I had so many voice mails to listen to—all of them horrible to hear. My mom, Nikki, and my three younger sisters, Margaret, Colleen, Connie. They had called me to yell at me about leaving Massachusetts and not telling them where I was and about a bunch of other idiotic garbage.

Three months and no phone calls from them and now they call. What?

My dad, Ryan, had called me next to tell me that he had sold my dog Max to the next-door neighbor without any hesitation or sympathy. He did not want my dog to be in his house anymore because I was not there to take care of my dog, and that he did not want the responsibility to take care of my dog and then he said I will talk to you later and then hung up the phone.

Then to top that off, my two younger brothers, Chris and Nick, called to tell me that my old boyfriend from high school, Fred Spearman, had been injured in a motorcycle accident and was asking for me.

The problem with that was Fred was suffering from memory loss as a result of the accident and that he was married. He had told the doctors and the nurses that I was his wife.

Grace, Fred's wife, called to tell me that she was confused about the whole wife thing at the hospital. She went on and on about how she had been at the wedding and she had said the vows and exchanged rings and that she was his wife and that I was not. She went on and on and would not stop.

She had the audacity to know if Fred and I were secretly married or were having an affair behind her back. Grace said that she thought her marriage to Fred had now been a complete and utter sham.

"Are you kidding me?" I said. I am so frustrated.

Stan called me last. "Mary Beth! This is Stan! Where are you? Did you quit? Why aren't you here at work? Is this your way of thanking me? You have not earned any vacation days yet Mary Beth. Mr. Mark Greenland wants your head on a plate and so do I. Call me back right away when you get this message." I decide to not call anybody back not even Stan.

Monday morning, I am back at work and on top of listening on Saturday afternoon to Friday's horrible phone messages, I came to find out about a scheme that involved Stan.

Stan and one of the senior partners Bill Goodale, were working late with me on Monday night. Some of the offices had windows open. The building is not a skyscraper. It is an independent building all on its own. Stan and Mr. Mark Greenland had built it this way. They did not want to be attached to any other building.

From my desk, I can hear the wind blowing steadily outside, and a thunderstorm is nearby.

Just then a piece of paper flew into my office and onto the floor by mistake. I had to walk over to one of my filling cabinets and I stepped on the piece of paper not realizing that it was anything of importance.

I do not care about anything at that moment. I just want to finish my work and go home. I walk back and sit at my desk.

When I am done with my work, I am so upset. I run my hands through my hair. I wish to scream out loud to myself from all the frustrations with Stan, my family, and my job and to everything else that is going wrong in my life.

I do not realize it, but I stand up from my desk and I actually scream out loud. I thought that I was the only one who had heard myself scream but Stan and Bill had heard me scream too.

Stan calls out from his office doorway, "Everything all right in there Mary Beth?"

I hear Bill say, "Quiet down Mary Beth. I am on the phone."

What? Stan cares. Who am I kidding? I shook my head. No, of course not. He does not care about anybody. And shut up Bill!

Stan is not asking me out of concern. It is more like a warning about how I am not even to think about having a bad day. Bill is probably on the phone trying to steal a client away from another firm or is planning some kind of illegal activities. Bill is always up to no good.

I look down at the floor and something catches my eye. I see a piece of paper which is right in front of my desk.

That is funny. That piece of paper was not there before.

I walk over to the front of my desk and I pick up the piece of paper. Where has this paper come from? Then I realize the wind must have blown it into my office. Something caught my eye while reading the piece of paper.

My back is to my office door. I was not paying any attention, so I did not hear Stan come into my office. "Did you happen to see a piece of paper with the company logo on it addressed to me from Mr. Mark Greenland?"

Stan scared me. I am so startled that I did not hear what he had said to me. I jump and I scream. I place the piece of paper underneath my desk calendar.

"What do you want Stan?" I said turning around to face him.

"Hello! Mary Beth, did you see the piece of paper or not? I am late for a date with my wife for drinks at the Carlisle."

I said to Stan with an attitude and through gritted teeth, "No. I have not seen your *stupid* piece of paper. Have a nice time with your wife. Goodnight." I turn my back to him. I am holding onto my desk so tightly that I do not realize that my knuckles have turned white. I am trying so hard not to walk over to Stan and punch him in the face.

I feel Stan's eyes on me even though my back is to him. I hear him run his hands through his hair. He sighs heavily. I think that he wants to say something to me, but he does not say anything. He turns and walks out of my office.

After I made sure that Stan was gone, I quickly pull the piece of paper out from underneath my desk calendar and start to read the piece of paper quietly to myself. I cannot believe what I am reading.

I read the piece of paper over and over again to be sure. Apparently, there is to be a meeting to be held soon with Stan, Doug, Mr. Mark Greenland, Harry Greenland and Bill Goodale next week with another firm. They are apparently all involved in serious illegal criminal activities that could ruin all of their careers and this firm.

They are threatening another firm to keep quiet. If this firm, that is not named, is to keep their secrets quiet, then Mr. Mark Greenland will not purchase their firm and put them out of business and instead he will offer them a business proposal of some kind, that also is not mentioned.

The firm has only two weeks to think it over.

Wow! This is big. Really big.

Oh gosh! I did not think this through.

What would Stan do to me if he found out that I knew about this?

CHAPTER 5

The next morning, I am sitting at my desk like usual, staring into Stan's office. I can see him. He is sitting in his chair. His door is wide open. He is clearly stressed out about something. He keeps running his hand over his mouth, his chin and through his hair.

Does he know? Did he find out? What is he thinking? He must know. I am a goner. I know it. The phone rang. Stan turned to look at me right then like he had sensed me looking at him. Stan did not pick up his phone, then I realize that it is my phone that is ringing. Oh no. Oh gosh.

I quickly look away from him and I pick up my phone. I am so nervous and jittery. I have to ask whoever it is to repeat themselves several times. I cannot believe what I am hearing. The person on the phone starts to get impatient with me. I finally get myself under control and could speak again. I am in shock. I take a deep breath.

"I am so sorry. Could you repeat what you just said again?" I asked.

"My name is Kim Meadows. I am calling from a firm in Coast Grove, Massachusetts. Our firm is called Courtland, Woodhall and Frankland. We found your résumé in our mailbox about a month ago and we have finally found the time to contact you. I see that you used to live and work here in Massachusetts before. Would you consider moving back here to Massachusetts? Are you available to interview if you are interested?"

"Yes, I am interested in interviewing with your firm. I have all next week open," I said this without thinking. I am way too excited.

"We would like to finish interviewing by next Friday." Do you have a specific day and time in mind?" said Kim.

I cannot remember when I had sent my resume out to anybody after what happened at my last job.

I look up just then still trying to remember how I applied to this firm and then Stan appears. He is standing in my doorway.

He must have been listening to my phone conversation. Oh no. How long has he been standing there?

The look on Stan's face is not good. I stop talking to Kim. I suddenly turn away from Stan's glare and his piercing eyes, like how dare I leave him and this firm and find another place to work.

I do not care at the moment, so I get up from my desk and tell Kim to hold on for a moment. I put the phone down on my desk and walk over to my office door and I close the door right in Stan's face.

Take that Stan! In your face!

The look on Stan's face as I am closing my office door on him is priceless. I cannot help but smile a little and laugh at his expense. Good riddance. It is about time that I think about myself and not him.

I think I heard Stan say something to me through the door—that he is coming back to talk to me. I do not care. I am happy. I did a little dance.

Yes! You did it Mary Beth!

You stood up to him!

Then I remember about Kim being on the phone, so I hurry back to sit at my desk. I pick up the phone and I said to Kim with confidence in my voice and a big smile on my face, "I am so sorry Kim for the delay in my response. I would like to come in on Wednesday of next week at 3:00pm if that would be okay."

Kim said, "Great. That should be fine. I will call you back to confirm that the time and date that you prefer to interview with us works with Mr. Courtland's, Mr. Woodhall's and Mr. Frankland's schedule. What time do you normally leave for the day?"

Oh my gosh. I had no idea how to answer her question. What do I tell her?

I lived, ate and breathed here. I never left the firm at a normal business hour. Maybe I will just get up and leave at 5:00pm today. Yes. That sounds good. I will do just that. In your face Stan.

I said to Kim, "I leave work at 5:00pm today. I just want to say thank you Kim for taking the time to reach out and call me about this position. I look forward to hearing from you later on today. Thank you again. Oh, wait Kim, could you tell me what is the position that I will be interviewing for? You forgot to mention it."

Kim replied, "Oh of course. Sorry Mary Beth that I forgot to mention that. The position that you will be interviewing for will be for a senior partner and will be located in our mergers and acquisitions department."

"Mary Beth, I have to say you are one lucky person to work at a firm that lets you leave at 5:00pm. Sorry for you not letting you know before about the open position. I will try and call you back before 5:00pm today. Mary Beth, may I say that it was a pleasure speaking with you just now. Goodbye." Kim hung up.

I hung up the phone too. I breathe a sigh of relief. Maybe this new firm will pay me more. Maybe I will be able to make partner this time around. Maybe there will be a good person at the firm who can be my mentor and give me the respect that I deserve. Oh, the possibilities! I feel so relieved. I can feel the tension leave my body. My body feels so alive again after such a long time. It feels wonderful.

I am so excited that I feel like doing cartwheels down the hall in front of Stan's and Doug's offices.

I only hope that I will not be disappointed to work at this new firm. I hope that I will get the job. There is really nothing here in New York to make me stay.

It is only 1:00pm. I stop thinking nonsense and look at the piles of work on my desk and sigh.

I stand up from behind my desk to open my office door. I decide to take a walk. I do not want to sit behind my desk anymore.

I left my office and started to walk around. It feels good to stretch my legs. I got to see and to say hi to people that I have worked with a few times but have not seen since. The days have gone by in a flash.

I walk around the entire office building and make it back to my office but not before I go outside to enjoy the warm air and the sunshine for a bit. When I get back to my office, I look around—the walls, the floor, and my desk. I walk over to the only window in my office by my desk and open up the blinds. I stare out into the town to watch the busy city. All the people are bustling about their daily business. I start to remember the good times Stan and I had when we worked together back in Massachusetts. We would go to lunch or to dinner together and laugh, share good memories and funny stories along with a few kisses because we were in love and because we were drunk sometimes. The good old days.

We would let the moments run away with us. I smile and still wonder about him, about us. I make myself remember more of the good times we shared together. I smile bigger at every good memory and when I am done daydreaming, I turn around.

I am hoping to see him, thinking for a moment that he will change my mind and make me happy to stay, but Stan is not in his office. Stan is gone.

I am sad and then my stomach starts to hurt.

I finally realize that this is a dream that will not come true. Stan Howler cannot be a part of my future. My smile slowly fades away and a frown takes its place as I stand by the window and stare into Stan's empty office.

CHAPTER 6

Kim did call me yesterday. I was so excited to hear back from her. She said next Wednesday at 3:00pm would be fine. She said that everyone could not wait to meet me including Kim.

It sounds wonderful—too good to be true in fact. I am now wondering how on earth will I get the time off when I still have so much work to get done here and plus Stan is upset with me.

I am so excited thinking about my job interview that I went and told Rebecca that I will be going out of town next week for a job interview. I told her around lunch time about 1:00pm. Big mistake.

Rebecca told Stan by accident later on that afternoon around 3:00pm. Rebecca came to my office right afterwards to apologize to me, around 5:00pm but it was too late. She said that she was talking to Jenny Trinket from accounting about me and she did not happen to see Stan standing right there listening to their conversation about me. Stan went through the roof.

I was running around to my co-workers offices to drop paperwork off as well as packages because there were not enough people to help around the office that day. Quite a few people were still on vacation, so we were short staffed.

I had to go to meetings all day. I did not have much time to go to lunch let alone go to the bathroom.

It is starting to get dark outside by the time I am heading back to my office. It is later on in the evening about 8:00pm when it happened.

I am not paying attention. I am exhausted. I am preparing for my job interview in my head. I get back to my office and close the door but not all the way.

Someone walks into my office. I do not hear this person come into my office. The door shuts ever so quietly.

I am too busy trying to get everything organized and straightened up because my office is still a complete disaster from before.

The person slowly approaches me as I am separating papers at my desk. My back is to this person. I am reading and rereading and checking to make sure I put each piece of paper into the correct folder.

Oh help. How am I supposed to fix this mess?

I throw my hands up in anguish. I am so upset and frustrated.

Suddenly, I hear a noise that is quite close to me. I instantly stop sorting out the papers and listen ever so carefully.

I come to realize that the sound is someone breathing, and it is not my own. I stand completely still. After a few minutes I smell something. I could not remember, but the smell is very familiar. It is on the tip of my tongue. Too much information is running through my mind at the time.

It is too late. I am caught totally off guard. Then all I see is black.

When I wake up, I am lying on my side almost fully on my stomach. I think there was a blackout because the lights to my office were turned off, but then I can see light through my office door from the hallway. I can hear people talking.

I am totally winded. I am having problems breathing. I am in a lot of pain. I have no idea why I am on the floor. How did I get on the floor? All the papers I have worked so hard on to organize into the folders are all over the place again.

What? How did this happen?

That is when I see them. I see shoes—brown shoes. I smell the cologne. Someone's hands are on my body. I can feel where they are—on my arms, on my shoulders, on my chest. Someone is running their hands through my hair!

Suddenly, I turn onto my back and yell, "Ow!" I feel an excruciating pain run through my entire body. Then I feel something hard on my stomach—a foot, a shoe pressing on my stomach. A shoe pressing hard with a lot of pressure on my stomach.

I hear a voice. The voice is unkind. "What I have done for you Mary Beth, can never be repaid. I have gone out on a limb for you. I have put my job and my career on the line for you. And this is the thanks that I get?" Stan is pressing his foot into my stomach even harder. I can feel like my spleen is being ruptured. I am in so much pain. I try to move. I try to break free, but I cannot. He is too strong.

I yell, "Get off me. You're hurting me, Stan. Get your foot off my chest. Now!"

Someone must have heard me because there is a knock on the door. It is Gregory Kitts from litigation. I am so relieved. I said, "Come in," as loudly as I could muster.

Stan took his foot off my chest and helped me up. "Get up and go to the door," he said.

I had trouble standing up straight. I am wincing in pain. I manage to go to the door to talk to Greg.

"Hi, Greg. How are you? Perfect timing." I reach the door before Greg could fully open it.

I use the door for support. I am clutching my chest. Great—another night at the ER. The staff knew me by my first name by now. I am sure of it.

"Hi, Mary Beth. I am good. How are you? I heard loud noises. Is everything alright in here? I see you have no lights on in your office."

"I am fine, Greg. I am just yelling at my computer in the dark."

I am just about to tell Greg about Stan. Stan came from behind me and whispered in my ear, "Do not let him know that I am here or else!"

I flinch at the sound of Stan's voice. "Oh, don't worry Greg, everything is fine. I like working in the dark. It keeps me calm. Thank you for checking up on me. I appreciate it."

Greg said, "Okay, Mary Beth." He looked around my office. "Have a good night." He did not seem to notice that Stan was hiding behind the door. If he did, he did not let on.

"Thanks, Greg. Have a good night."

"Thank you, Mary Beth." He waved to me and then Greg turned and walked down the hallway. I wanted to keep the door open, but Stan pushed it closed knocking me out of the way.

Stan turned on the lights to my office. He moved away from me to other side of my office. He turned his back to me. He is clearly mad. His breathing is heavy. He starts talking to me. "Oh, I am so mad at you Mary Beth."

"What on earth for? What have I done to you? If anyone should be mad it should be me mad at you. I should press charges against you for assaulting me just now."

"But you won't. I know you won't." Stan turned to face me and looked me in the eye and pointed his finger at me. "I know you too well Mary Beth to do any such thing because you are in love with me, and you would not do that to me. It will hurt *my* reputation. And what will it do to yours? It will make me look bad. I could lose my job. I know about your interview next week—with my rival, Courtland, Woodhall, and Frankland. Do not dare cross me Mary Beth. I am your friend. Courtland, Woodhall, and Frankland is a rival to this firm and to me. How dare you? And you know it and that is what makes me *furious.*" Stan's voice got louder and louder as he talked.

What? A rival? A friend? What is he talking about?

Stan must be on drugs because the last two months his behavior towards me has been appalling. What happened at the firm Courtland, Woodhall, and Frankland that made them his rival? Why would Stan think that I knew anything about this? What is wrong with him? He is acting crazy.

I do not want to be in the same room as him anymore. I cannot stand to be anywhere near him. I do not want to look at him let alone talk to him. I want to get away from him.

A friend? What friend? What is he talking about? Who is he kidding? He must be insane. He does not even know what a friend is.

I muster up the courage to approach Stan. I have to hold onto the side of my body where Stan just hurt me. I want to get right up into his face.

It takes me a few minutes to hobble over to him, but then I get right into his face and I look him right in his eyes and yell, "Stan, you stupid nerf ball. I do not love you anymore. You do not respect me at all. I do not love cowards. What makes you think that I will not call the cops? You do not control me, Stan. Now… Get Out!"

CHAPTER 7

Stan did not leave my office. He stood motionless right in front of my face. He stared into my eyes and said nothing. Everything right now is a blur of emotions for me. There is so much tension in the air between us. I can feel it. Could Stan feel it too?

Stan is in shock. I shocked Stan. Who could have thought I could do that to him? It is always Stan shocking me. Whatever I said to him had made him extremely angry.

Before I could move away from Stan, he grabbed my face and pulled me to him and then pressed his lips to mine. He grabbed my shoulders and squeezed them hard and slammed me up against the wall closest to my desk. His lips never left mine.

I need to come up for air, but he will not let me. He held me like this forever it felt like. Finally, his lips left mine.

His breath was heavy on my face. His breath smelled of peppermint candy. His cologne was Polo by Ralph Lauren—my favorite. I always believed he had started to wear it because I had told him that it was my favorite men's cologne.

His arms were like a vice around my shoulders. His body is pressed heavily up against me. I am pinned up against the wall. I am breathing heavy and so is Stan.

Stan finally released me, but he did not turn and leave my office. He stood right in front of me.

"What in the world was that for? You had no right to do that. How dare you!" I said to Stan with so much disgust in my voice. I am so mad at Stan that I try and slap him.

Stan was ready for me. He stepped back and away from me and grabbed my arm and pushed it away from his face so fast.

He breathed heavy for a minute. He looked right at me. Stan pointed his finger at me. He said, "You pissed me off. I have—had feelings for you Mary Beth. I stand corrected. I have feelings for you. You are the only person who makes sense to me. I cannot let you go. I do not want to let you go. I do not want you out of my life. Every time I see you it brings me pain."

What? Where did that come from?

Stan walks towards me and stops when he is close to me. He reaches out his arms to me and gently pulls me into his embrace. I do not fight him on this. I think that he is going to kiss me again.

Stan ran his hands through my hair and down my cheek. He separated us a little bit, but he still held me close.

He looked down at me and said, "Remember the one night that we were together. It really was magical. And you know, it makes me so angry Mary Beth that you can never be mine."

Oh, those hypnotizing eyes of his, but then his expression changed like lightening. Stan looked at me differently and with such anger and then he violently released me and pushed me up against the wall. "Get out of my face Mary Beth," Stan said to me as he turned and walked towards the door.

"You first," I shout at Stan. "I have always been willing to wait for you Stan. I have so much love and respect for you. You have given me no answer. All that I have gotten from you is your look of disgust, like you are always disappointed in me. Like there is always something wrong with me and that I cannot do anything right in your eyes. That nothing that I say or do is ever good enough for you. Take a good look at me Stan for *I am* in so much pain." I start to ache with pain in my shoulders and on the side of my body where Stan had hurt me. I try to massage both my shoulders and the side of my body to stop the pain, but my body hurts too much.

What is the use? The pain will not go away. The pain will not stop. I let out a heavy sigh and put my head up against the wall and I look up to the ceiling and I curl my arms around my body to try to shield myself from Stan.

I can hear Stan's footsteps on the carpet. He is walking away from me and then there was no sound.

What? Did he listen to what I just said to him? Did he hear my cries of pain? Did he hear me sigh just now?

I force myself to look at the door. Stan's hand is on the doorknob. He is about to open the door and leave, but then he stops. He lets go of the doorknob. He turns to look at me. His face has softened. His facial expression now seemed more of regret than anger.

I cannot believe that he just assaulted me and in the way that he did, with such force and with such anger. I will not forget about this. How can I?

Being treated badly is like a bad dream. It scares you too much and it does not goes away. You cannot forget about it… ever.

Stan approached me slowly and when he got close enough to me, he placed his hands on the wall, one hand on each side of my face.

Stan looks deep into my eyes. His eyes travel up and down my body. He notices that I have my hands curled around my body.

Stan put his hands to my face and starts to caress both of my cheeks. He is too quick for me to react and I let him. I close my eyes and I lower my head down towards the floor. I cannot not look into his eyes.

I have to be strong now. If I look into his eyes, he will see right through me and I will become so weak.

Stan's breath is on my face. He gently pulls me into his embrace again, he put his arms around me and hugs me tight. "I am so sorry Mary Beth. My emotions got the best of me. Please forgive me. Please do not hate me."

Trouble—oh no, trouble. My emotions are in shambles. I do not want to be that woman. I want to be strong, but I cannot be strong when I am feeling like this.

"I do not know what to think anymore Stan. I have been thinking that there was never an us. I feel like this whole time—everything between us—has just been all lies. I am sorry." I can feel that my tears are close. I can hear the strain in my voice. I am close to breaking down and I do not want to. No. Not in front of Stan. I cannot let myself fall apart. Not now.

Stan grabs my shoulders and pushes me back a bit and holds me at arm's length. A few minutes later, he takes my hands into his hands and squeezes them lightly. I can feel his eyes on me.

Stan lets go of my hands. I feel him place his hands on each side of my head. He tilts my head up to force me to look up at him. "Mary Beth, I cannot believe you just said that to me. Was I not honest with you from the beginning? I let you in." He grabs both my shoulders and shakes me a little. "I let you get close to me. I was going to leave my wife for you Mary Beth. I wanted my wife to see that. I wanted her to see you with me. I wanted my wife to know that I chose you."

Huh? What is Stan talking about? I start to remember the past and I smile. Then a frown replaces my smile on my face because here we are arguing about us… again.

"What are you talking about Stan? This is all news to me," I said.

Stan got quiet. He pushed my hair away from my face, tucked it behind my ear. Then he whispered into my ear, "What we had was definitely real. It was. I felt a connection then and I still do. And now I feel like you are drifting away from me again. Where are you going? You are my life. You are my dreams—my dream. Do not go Mary Beth. Please do not go."

Stan looked deep into my eyes again. I have to look at him. I cannot look away now. What is he going to do next? What is he thinking?

Stan placed his hands on each side of my mouth right down at my jawline. Stan pulled my face towards him. He kissed me on my lips ever so lightly.

His kiss felt like heaven. Oh, how I have missed his sweet and gentle kisses. Oh, how his kisses were like volcanic eruptions to my body. Oh, the memories. Those feelings that I used to have for him are coming back again. It is too soon for me. I am not ready yet.

I remember them so well now. This is not a good thing. I have to stop him. But how?

I feel his hands let go of mine. He grabs my wrists and places my arms down at my sides. I feel his hands go up and down my arms and then slowly his hands make their way to my stomach. He starts to massage the side of my body where he had hurt me.

I wince in pain. "Ow. Stan stop that hurts." I try to push his hands away. He grabs both of my hands and places both my arms behind my back with one hand and with his other hand he puts his finger to my lips.

"Hush Mary Beth. Stay still. Do not move," he whispered in my ear ever so softly.

CHAPTER 8

I stayed still, whether out of fear of giving him a reason to hurt me again or out of sheer pleasure of knowing what might be coming next. The thought of his wife and that he is a married man and everything for that matter, I just push it into the back of my head for the moment.

Stan and I have not been alone in a long time and I have missed his touch and his kisses.

Stan moved us to the front of my desk.

"I forgot how you felt. Your skin is so soft. I want you, Mary Beth. You smell wonderful. I want to drink you in." Stan took a deep breath and breathed me in. He smelled my hair. He smelled my neck. He smelled my skin right where my blouse was open, right above my décolleté. His breathing hitched. His voice got deeper and quieter as Stan whispered to me in my ear, "I want you, Mary Beth. I have to have you. I want you on your messy desk right now."

Stan started to touch me and then he started to gently kiss my cheeks, my lips, and my neck. His lips and his touch feel so good that I start to moan loudly. I totally forgot that the walls and the doors are not thick.

My voice possibly traveled down the hall so everyone who is in the building right now can hear what is going on in my office.

"I like your touch, Stan. Your touch feels so good. Your kisses are wonderful. Do not stop. Please do not stop," I said.

I really am enjoying myself and I should not be enjoying myself.

I forgot everything for a moment. His touch and his kisses feel so good. I start to touch him slowly. He starts to growl.

Stan lowered me to my desk. He leans over me and says in my ear, in a hoarse whisper, "Lay back on your desk. That's a good girl. Now hike up your skirt for me Mary Beth. I want control Mary Beth. Let me take control."

My whole body jumped right then. I finally woke up and came back to reality. I sit up straight on my desk so fast and try to wiggle my way out of his arms, but I cannot. He would not let me go. I start to feel dizzy and lightheaded. I swear that I am seeing stars right now.

I am totally freaking out. I want to run away from him, but I stay right in his arms instead. I put my face into his chest.

What is going on? What is wrong with me? Oh my gosh! What am I doing? What am I thinking? I cannot do this!

I move my head away from his chest so I can breathe. I said out loud, "Whore!"

I put my head down into my hands. I am so ashamed of how weak he can make me feel.

"What? Who are you calling a whore?" Stan said. "Me," I said so quietly that he had to pick my head up to hear me.

"I am calling myself a whore. What am I doing here alone with you in my office? I dislike you. I dislike that you can make me feel so good inside and that my mind runs away with the moment. This is complete torture. I cannot do this with you anymore. I feel like this whole seduction scene or whatever you want to call it is a lie. There I said it."

Stan looked at me and studied my face for a few minutes before shaking his finger no. Stan slowly helped me up from my desk. He closed his arms around my whole body and then he pulled me close to him again. He kissed my forehead and my lips so gently.

I let myself go. I relaxed my entire body and leaned into Stan. I closed my eyes.

We stayed in each other arms and occasionally made out.

Wow! It is really late. It is 2:00am! We both reluctantly released each other even after realizing what time it is.

Stan did not speak one word to me after he released me from his arms. He turned and left my office, but then he came back into my office a few minutes later. He stood inside of my doorway with his briefcase in one of his hands facing me with a slight smile on his face.

He held out his hand for me. I placed my hand into his hand, and he squeezed my hand. We walked out of my office and the building hand in hand.

We hugged and kissed each other good night in the parking lot and then we went home separately.

∿

The next morning at work, things were different. Stan was warm and bubbly to me. He spoke softly to me when we saw each other. We exchanged pleasant hellos and good mornings. He smiled that brilliant smile at me and I smiled back at him. Then throughout the day he blew me a kiss every time he saw me when no one was looking. I glowed all the way back to my office each time.

The first time Stan blew me a kiss, I walked into a wall on the way back to my office. The second time Stan blew me a kiss I ended up walking straight into the men's bathroom and having to explain myself to Mr. Mark Greenland. Oops! I saw Stan from laughing at me from a far.

I was in my office and it was about 2:00pm when I heard a knock on the door to my office.

I heard this sensual and husky voice say, "I thought about you all last night, Mary Beth. You were wonderful to touch, to smell, and to taste. I hope we can do that again sometime soon—like maybe tonight. My wife is going to an important business dinner. What do you say?"

It is Stan was at my office door. His voice is soft and sensual.

I was so busy at my computer that I did not get a chance to look up at him. I was listening to him though—to his every word. Oh, yes. I was. I am hooked. My lips start to salivate. My body starts to respond to his voice. I am going to give Stan my answer when I look up at the door. Stan is gone.

What? Where did he go?

Stan did not wait for my answer. I am being tormented. He is tormenting me on purpose. I am stuck between pleasure and pain. I start to pout.

Stan is trying to make me stay. I cannot let him do this to me. If I get this job in Massachusetts, I can start a new life and get away from him—from his seduction. If I stay, it will just end up in turmoil. I just know it.

I knew it from the beginning. He flirted, and I swooned. I fell into his clutches. Now, I am stuck between a rock and a hard place.

What if Stan sabotaged my career? What if Stan or anybody else from this job tells lies about me? What will I do then? Oh, gosh. I shudder to think about it.

There are so many hours still left at the office. If Stan does not come over to my office, then I will be safe—for the time being. I think.

It is 7:00pm and still no sign of Stan. What a liar! What a crock! I decide to pack up my things and go home.

I grab my coat, purse, keys and briefcase. I swing my purse over my shoulder. I push in my chair and straighten out my desk a little bit. I turn off the lights to my office and I walk out the door.

As I am leaving, I see a light in both Stan and Doug's office but there is no sign of either of them.

Who cares? I finally get into my car—a brand-new white Buick. I bought it when I got the job here. I had been so proud of myself. I still am, but many things still haunt me—things that do not make any sense to me about Stan. I finally arrive at my house. I like it. It is cozy. I walk into my house and slam the front door shut. I forget to lock the front door. I am so preoccupied with what chores that I have to do around the house. I am not paying any attention to anything else. Plus, I am so exhausted from Stan playing with my emotions and all the late nights at the office.

Now onto bigger problems. My large white kitchen is in ruins—too much bad wine. Well, it had not been bad when I was drinking it to be honest. It actually tasted surprisingly good.

Pizza boxes and other takeout food containers litter my kitchen counters and my kitchen floor. It is a mess everywhere.

I take off my coat, walk over to my coat closet and hang up my coat. As I am taking my keys out of my coat pocket, I hear a noise outside, like a car, but I am too tired to go over to the window and look outside to see what the noise is.

I turn and walk up the stairs to my bedroom and turn on the lights. I put my keys into my purse and put down my purse and briefcase on one of my chairs located next to my bed.

I walk over to my windows and pull down the shades and close the curtains.

I change out of my work clothes. I just throw them all over the floor. I will deal with it later. I change into my pajamas, bathrobe and slippers. I turn off the light to my bedroom and head downstairs to the kitchen.

I come downstairs and pass by my living room. I have to go into the kitchen and start cleaning up now. My kitchen is such a mess, and it smells too. I am thinking to myself. If I do not care about my virtues or myself, then I will sleep with Stan. I will surrender my body—my whole self—to him, but Stan is wrong. He cannot have me. He is a married man.

I have other important things to think about right now and Stan cannot be one of them. I cannot think of Stan right this instant. I have other things to think about like cleaning my kitchen, doing the dishes and drinking my bad wine.

CHAPTER 9

Suddenly, I hear something. What is that noise? As I am picking things up off my kitchen floor, I stop. I stay completely still.

I hear the noise again. This time the noise is alerting me to the fact that someone is in my living room. Oh my gosh!

Someone is in my house! Who can it be?

I slowly stand up from the kitchen floor and walk over to the front door. I find it to be closed and locked. Weird. How did whoever was here get in? Is it just one person? Are there more?

Oh, gosh. I walk back to the kitchen to call 9-1-1, but Stan stops me cold.

I freeze in place. My mouth drops open. I cannot believe it. Stan followed me home. He scared me. He violated my trust. He trespassed into my home! My own sense of security!

My home is the only security that I have. I try to scream. I want to run away from Stan, but I cannot move.

Stan is clearly drunk. I can tell. He has that drunk look in his eyes. I know that drunk look. I remember.

He clearly has been drinking for a while. I can smell the alcohol on him, and I can no longer smell his cologne. It is so overpowering. I put my arm up to my nose to stop breathing it in.

I should not be scared. I should be shouting at him, but I cannot say anything. I am totally silent. It would all be too simple for him to think that I would succumb to his charms, to his touch right now.

I want Stan to touch me so badly though. I feel something inside of me. What on earth is it about Stan that makes me feel so hot and bothered? I am so confused. I should be so angry at him. I should kick his ass out.

Right now, Mary Beth, kick him out. I cannot. Who was the coward now?

"I was waiting for you at the office Mary Beth. I cannot believe you left the office. I told you not to leave. I told you that I would come for you," Stan said to me with anger in his voice while shaking his finger at me. "I came back to work after a meeting, only to find you leaving the office. Why? Why did you leave? Why are you leaving me? Why did you leave me all alone? I thought we talked about this. I thought we were good—that everything was good between us last night. I thought that we had a mutual understanding. I made dinner reservations at 8:00pm for just the two of us and now I have to cancel them." He threw his arms up in the air.

Stan kept talking, but I cannot believe my ears. He was forcing me into a sexual relationship/affair, giving me no choice in the matter…again. Has he forgotten that he is married? Has he forgotten that he has kids to think about?

I know what he is thinking about, and it is not a good idea, but given this is Stan, he will ask me. He will always ask me first. He will not take what is not his, but this time I feel it is different.

I am not sure of how to control the situation because this time around I think that my body really wants him. I really think that Stan has the control over me this time.

As Stan continues to talk to me while slurring his words, he starts undressing himself right in front of me in my own kitchen, as if he were in his own bedroom in his own house with his wife.

He made his way through my kitchen and placed his coat and his suit jacket on one of the chairs at my kitchen table.

He loosened his tie and took it off and placed it on top of his coat and suit jacket.

Gee what was next? This left truly little to the imagination.

He kept on talking to me like we were man and wife and we had kids. It was like my home was his, and he owned it. His shoes were next, along with his socks. Wow, his socks gave off a really bad smell, adding to the bad wine and the takeout food floating through my house. I almost passed out onto the floor. How many times could this man make me faint? Stan must be trying to a break record.

I am not really listening to him talk. I am more concerned about what will happen next when he starts to unbutton his shirt or undo his belt and unzip his pants. I suddenly felt turned on by him.

I just stood there in fear, in my own house no less. I am paralyzed. Is this the Stan that I know? He is clearly different—drunk and stupid. His tone is nasty and mean. He is scolding me over and over again about me leaving the office and saying that he cannot understand why things had gone bad so fast when they were so good just the other night.

He was blaming me for everything—including things that had nothing to do with me. I did not work for his bank and screw up his bank account. I did not ring up his groceries at the grocery store and overcharge him. I did not hit his car and take off.

What is this about? Why is he so angry with me? His voice is getting louder and louder. I am getting really scared now. What should I say to Stan? How can I make him calm down? Should I move around him, or should I stay still? I have no idea at this point.

I am getting quite fed up with his crap. It is not my fault. He has had every opportunity, like me, to stop this from forming into something else—into a jumble of emotions that are seriously getting out of hand.

I feel like going over to him and punching and slapping him across the face. I also want to go over to Stan and give him a hug and a kiss all at the same time.

1, 2, 3...punch, kick, slap, hug, kiss. I can do it.

Maybe his wife and kids did not love him, but I am not responsible for his feelings. I am not responsible for the lack of love or for his emotional state. That is his wife's job. Why am I stuck with it?

Enough. I have had enough. Okay. Here goes. I am going to do this in one fell swoop. Only time would get it right.

I finally get the nerve to walk over to him while still listening to him yell and carry on. When I get up to his face, I stare into his eyes that I can see are full of anger and are also blood shot red. He looks like he is going to puke all over me, but then I put my arms around him and give him a hug regardless.

I cannot believe this. Stan instantly shut up. Gee, I should do this more often. What a baby! I start to hug him harder, but then he belched, and I felt his stomach move. Big mistake. I should have punched and slapped him first.

I let go of Stan and I look at him. He asks me where the bathroom is. I told him where it is, and he walks off in a hurry.

I go back to cleaning my kitchen. I am finishing up as Stan comes back from the bathroom. He walks over to me and stands next to me at the kitchen sink.

"Are you alright? Did you vomit? Would you like some water?" I ask Stan.

"Yes. I just made it to the toilet. There's a little bit of a mess in the bathroom that I did not clean up."

Stan looks at me, rubs his hands together, and then he licks his lips. "So," he said, "now where were we? Oh, right. You gave me a hug and now where is my kiss, Mary Beth?"

Stan got closer to me while I was at the sink still trying to wash the dishes. He acts like nothing happened—like he had not just vomited all over my bathroom floor and had been yelling at me at the top of his lungs just a few minutes ago. I shake my head. I said to Stan, "Really Stan? Unbelievable."

CHAPTER 10

I cannot believe that this is happening to me.

Stan is standing so close to me at the kitchen sink. The hot water is running. He stares at me, and I stare back at him. I cannot speak, and it seems he cannot speak either. I seriously do not know what to say. I stop washing the dishes and turn the water off.

Suddenly Stan spoke. "I have loved you ever since you walked through the doors to the firm for your interview back in Massachusetts. I have never met anyone who is interviewing for a position in the lobby. Someone always does that for me, but something about you told me to meet you in the lobby. When I first met you, I wanted to be with you and have you all to myself and sweep you away— to try and persuade you to be mine. Then my wife came back into my life and told me that we were not splitting up. She changed her mind. She would come by the office and see me with you, and she would become jealous. At first, she was doing it just to keep tabs on me and make me mad, but then she really felt love for me again. I did not want to believe it at first, but then I realized she was telling me the truth. Now *you* might be leaving me. I feel so hollow inside. I got into a rage. I am so depressed. I do not want to lose you. My wife is now back in my life and taking up so much of my time. Can you please forgive me?"

Stan is so drunk, and he is slurring his words. He has vomit on his face, and at the same time he is trying so hard to be romantic.

I am appalled. He smelled bad and now here he is trying to blame me but making excuses at the same time.

Is he lying to me? Can I trust him again? I do not know. His apology is pathetic and half-assed, but what girl in love will not believe it.

What a fool Mary Beth! Do not be stupid!

I said to Stan, "I understand what you are trying to say to me, but I am not sure I totally 100 percent believe everything that you are telling me. I do not know what to believe anymore. I want to believe you Stan. I really do. I want to be in your life again and I want you back in mine. I want to stay here with you, but it would be for all of the wrong reasons. You have to see why."

I have no idea what it was that I said, but without any warning Stan attacked me.

He knocked me backwards and then pushed me up against the refrigerator. My head started spinning out of control. Now I feel really sick to my stomach. How can I go through this again?

I feel like throwing up. My chest area was starting to hurt again from where he had hurt me. I want to scream. He was kissing me and pressing himself against me.

Stan really is stupid. He is not thinking straight. He is moving too fast. Before I could protest, Stan swept me off my feet, and then walked to the stairs.

Wait! Hold up! My bedroom! Is there something wrong with this picture? Maybe he just wants to cuddle. Maybe he just wants love. Simple love. Is there a simple kind of love with men? No way. I do not think so. Yelling and sex is not communication. Maybe it is for him, but it is not for me.

I ask Stan as he is carrying me up the stairs, "Where are we going? Are you taking me to my bedroom? I was wondering why you were taking so long in the bathroom. You were checking out my place out, weren't you? Thinking about what you would do to me if I said yes and forgave you. Am I right?" I was so nervous to have asked him that.

Stan did not answer me at first, so I thought he had not heard me.

I was about to ask him again, but then he spoke, "Maybe you're right."

Stan got quiet again.

We reach my bedroom and he walks through the open door. He walks over to my bed and puts me down on my feet and makes me stand up straight. He grabs my wrist and turns me around so my back is to him. He takes off my bathrobe slowly and then he throws it on the floor right next to the bed. He walks over to the wall and turns on the lights.

I crawl across my bed to my nightstand and to get some tissues to wipe the vomit off of my mouth that Stan had slobbered over me when he had kissed me in the kitchen.

As soon as the lights come on, Stan as fast as he could unzippers his pants, takes them off, and drops them to the floor. Then he unbuttons his shirt and throws his shirt on top of his pants. So now he is only left wearing his white undershirt and his dark blue boxer shorts.

I turn around on my bed a few minutes later and sit up. I am completely shocked.

So gross and disgusting. What just happened here? Where are his clothes? How can a man get undressed that fast? I cannot get down to the bottom of my purse that fast.

Before I could move away from Stan, he grabs my feet and my ankles and pulls me down the bed, so I was at the foot of the bed where he is standing. He pushes me down on the bed when I try to sit up. I am panting and sweating, and my breathing is quickening. I swear he can hear my heartbeat.

I cannot make myself do this. I cannot live with myself if I have sex with a married man again, especially Stan. Stan will not stop. He is all over me. He will not stop kissing me and touching me all over. He is trying to take off my pajama bottoms, pressing and rubbing his body against me at the same time. His hands are all over my body. He is desperately trying to push my knees apart. My body is liking everything that he is doing but my mind is screaming stop this is wrong!

I want to kick him in the crotch, but I cannot move. His touch feels so good. He pins me down on the bed with his body. Every time I try to move or squirm, he puts more weight on top of me, pinning my arms down next to my sides. He kisses my neck ever so gently and starts to rub my breasts. I want to pop a tic tack into his mouth. His breathe smells so bad.

He is kissing my neck and rubbing my body with his expert hands when he suddenly farts loudly. He stops touching me. He looks at me. I look at him. Then a few seconds later, he burps so loud right into my face and laughs out loud like it is a funny joke or something.

I am so sick and disgusted. The romance is over. I do not want him to touch me any longer as I was just about to give into him. Oh my gosh!

"Get off me right now Stan! I am so disgusted by you. You are taking advantage of me, not because you are drunk but because you can. You are pinning me down and putting your hands all over my body and gripping me like a vise. That's not making love. That is forcing me to do something that I do not want to do. You are married, and I am not. We are not married. You are. I will not let this happen a second time."

Stan released his grip on me but did not get off me. He looks me straight into my eyes. Stan slowly puts his hand to my face and strokes my cheek.

"Tell me something that I don't know. Who cares? This is why I have to have you, Mary Beth. I can rival you up. You know how to make me want you so bad. Anyways. Who cares about my wife? Who cares if we have sex? It is just sex. She will never know if you and I do not tell her. I cannot let you go. You cannot leave me. I will not let you go. You are mine Mary Beth. You should know that by now."

"You are only saying this Stan because you are drunk. You do not mean any of it. Your breathe smells and your body smells even worse. You need to take a shower before I vomit all over you. And I care! What if I get pregnant? What then? What will you do then? Leave your wife and kids for me?"

Stan grabs my shoulders and pulls me right up into his face. He is serious. "Do you want my baby Mary Beth? Is that what you are telling me? Because if that is the case, I will gladly give it to you. You know I will." He stares at me and will not let go of my shoulders. He looks directly through me. I start to shiver. I start to lose control of myself.

Stan felt me start to shake and shiver. "Is this your body's way of an invitation to have sex with me Mary Beth? How about sex in the shower with you? That is quite romantic. Will that *do* it for you? Why didn't you say so? I am in a great mood for sex with you. Just say the word. Bedroom Sex. Shower sex. We can do one or both. Great idea, Mary Beth. I know that this was one of the many reasons why I hired you."

He looks so smug saying these words to me, but the room smelled of vomit, farts, and wine. How grotesque. He started to grind and press his body into me, and it hurt.

"You're hurting me, Stan. Get off me. I cannot feel my legs you dumb ass. You are clearly not romantic. I do not want to have sex with you—not in the shower, not on the roof, not on the stairs, or any other place else for that matter."

Stan finally rose slowly off me and pulled me half up with him with one hand. Then he let go of my hand, so I was sitting up at the foot of the bed again. He stood over me and looked down at me. Then he wiped one of his hands over his mouth and face and the other one through his hair.

"I know you. I know you too well Mary Beth. This isn't over," looking directly at me, Stan said.

Stan was just staring at me for quite a while with a hungry look in his eyes. He turned around suddenly and headed into the bathroom. Once inside the bathroom, he turned on the lights and shut the door behind him.

I sat on my bed looking at the closed bathroom door and then put my head in my hands.

What am I going to do?

These cravings that I have for Stan are truly maddening.

Can I really fight these feelings that I have for Stan?

How much longer can I go on without resisting Stan Howler?

CHAPTER 11

I am sitting in the middle of my bed curled up into a ball with my knees tucked into my chest. I close my eyes as I am listening to Stan take a shower in my bathroom, where I was not. He is singing so off key that I am sure if the birds outside could hear him, they would find a way to fly into my house and poop on his head.

I could have made love to Stan here on my bed and then had some more fun with him in the shower.

Could I be one of those people who just did not care at all?

About anything?

No, I could not be.

I am so tempted to take my pajamas off and jump into the shower with him. I have to take a shower anyway.

I am debating. Is there truly a correct answer to this situation?

I stood up from the bed and walked over to the bathroom door. I opened the bathroom door. Stan could not see or hear me. He is too busy grooming himself—*taking care of himself*—to notice me.

Would it be like that? Would he please himself and not me? Maybe it is a good idea to not sleep with him, but on the other hand I want to. The hot water is running. It is tempting, mighty tempting.

I close the bathroom door quietly. I walk up to the shower doors where Stan was inside showering. I just stood outside and stared through the heated and steam filled up shower doors. I watch his silhouette move around inside the shower doors, rinsing the shampoo and then the conditioner from his head. Then watching him put soap all over his body did not help me at all with my urges.

I was human, wasn't I? What was I doing standing here... alone outside looking in?

"Do you see anything that you like? I know you want to come in. *Do I tempt you, Mary Beth?*" I heard Stan say to me through the shower doors, bringing me out of my dream world right then and there.

How long had Stan been watching me? I jump. I quickly look down at the bathroom floor. After a few minutes, I slowly look up and our eyes lock.

His gaze pierces right into my chest. I cannot breathe. Without thinking, I take a deep breath, walk up to the shower doors, open them, and get into the shower with my pajamas on.

CHAPTER 12

Stan is watching me as I enter through the shower doors and offers his hand for me to help me into the shower. I do not take his hand. I pass by him, but not without touching his shoulder for support.

I stand at the back of the shower facing him with my head down. I can feel his eyes on me.

I am standing inside the shower and I am waiting. I do not know what is right or what is wrong at this point. Oh, what should I do?

I have to make a decision and—I want to touch Stan. I pick my head up and I take a few steps right up into his face. I brush my right hand over his right wet cheek with the back of my fingers. Stan closes his eyes as I start to touch his cheek. I put my lips close to his, but I did not press my lips against his. I am tempted.

I want to do this. I want to kiss him so badly. I can do this. I am breathing so hard.

Stan just stood there and he—is waiting. He is waiting for me to make a move. His eyes are still closed. This is my decision. It is up to me. I am happy that he knows that I have the kryptonite now and not him, but the sad part is I have no idea what to do next. I am not him. I am not a guy. I cannot just turn off my emotions and have sex. I have to do what is right. But for whom?

I can feel the warm water cascading and running down my body. My pajamas are soaking wet and are starting to become heavy. I look up and stare at him. I can feel the heat between us growing by the minute.

Stan broke the silence that was growing between us. His voice is husky and filled with want. He slowly opened his eyes and gazed at me like he was drinking me in. The look in his eyes made me melt all over. "What are you waiting for Mary Beth? Make a move."

I said, "I am thinking Stan. Ok. Just give me a minute."

Stan started to put his arms around me and to touch me while I was thinking. "I am not going to wait forever you know. Get naked with me right now while the water is still hot. You are wet, aren't you? I am not talking about your pajamas Mary Beth. I have lots of ideas of what I want you to do to me. You can only imagine what kinds of things I want to do to you. How many orgasms do you want tonight? I could make you really happy. It seems that you have forgotten that Mary Beth. Do you want me to remind you?"

Suddenly my brain shifts. What can I do for him? Haven't I done enough for him already? How much more do I have to do for you Stan? Seriously!

Buzzkill. Straight to my heart. I turn my body away from Stan and I start to pull the shower doors open.

He snatches my hand away from the shower doors and pushes them closed. He turns my face and my body around so that I am facing him. I am looking him straight into his eyes. He pulls me so close to his body and locks one his arms around my waist so I cannot escape. He grabbed one of my hands and turned my hand palm facing down and started to bring it slowly down from his neck to his rock-hard abs without ever breaking eye contact with me. He was totally silent as he continued to guide my hand downwards. His eyes showed so much heat in them that I thought that they would burn a whole through my chest. My heart is racing. He is driving me crazy. I am really trying to fight my urges. I am really trying to fight for control, but I am surely losing this battle.

He had my hand at his navel and started to push it down further. I did not pull my hand away. Do not ask me why. I swear he was testing me to see how far I can go without pulling my hand away.

"Do you feel how much I want you, Mary Beth? Do you know how much I desire you right now?" Stan was right in my ear saying these words to me. His voice is full of want. His words and that voice of his knocked me over. I feel such a hunger for him right now and it is not for food. What does he have over me? His words fill me with such want and need. I almost said yes.

I have to leave him but not before I kiss him. I am too needy not to. I have to leave the shower with what dignity I have left in me. I do not want to make a poor choice to only regret it later on. I do not want to get pregnant with Stan's child. I do not want him to control me and want sex with me again and again and again. I cannot be used like that. I refuse to be.

I pull my hand out of Stan's grasp. He actually let go of my hand but not without a fight. I grab his face and kiss him. One deep kiss. It is a wonderful feeling.

I release my hands from Stan's face. I slowly turn away from Stan and open the shower doors and close them as fast as I can—closing the doors to his beautiful face and his beautiful naked body.

My lips are burning from the kiss that I just stole from him. I place my finger to my lips. I want to kiss Stan again just like that. I yearn for him.

Stop it Mary Beth right now! Get a grip!

I lean up against the shower doors with my face lowered to the floor and my hands pressed up against the shower doors.

I pant and I try so hard to regain control of my breathing. I can feel Stan watching me. He is waiting, just waiting for me to return to him.

I look up slowly. He is taunting me with those piercing heated brown eyes. Full of want. Full of lust. I am feeling my own sense of want and lust, too. I feel the sensation drive a course through my body and I have to fight it.

I hear Stan say through the glass doors, "Mary Beth…I will have you again one day. I promise you that. One way or the other."

Oh no. Oh gosh. He meant it to. I have to leave my bathroom before he pulls me back inside the shower. And I know he will.

His words send chills up and down my spine. I slowly, very slowly, push myself away from the shower doors. I turn around and start to walk away. I am halfway across the bathroom when I hear Stan call my name so sensually that I stop in my tracks. I half turn around to see him. It took all of my self-control to not give into him.

I quickly run from the bathroom and shut the door. I cannot help but lean my back against the door. I sink to the floor slowly. I got away from him. I have no idea how.

I got away from his sensual words and his hot body. I swear that you can fry bacon on it. It is that hot.

Stan is my existence, but I cannot touch him. He is poison. A few moments ago, he had me feeling so good. A few minutes ago, oh my gosh, he almost had me. I cannot believe this.

I feel so lost. I feel so heartbroken. I was *so* into him. I was so in love with him at one point in my life.

What happened? I really thought that he was going to leave his wife for me. I felt it deep inside my bones.

Am I still in love with Stan, even after everything that he has put me through? I do not know what to feel anymore.

I hug myself tight and the tears start to fall.

I could still hear the water running from the shower through the closed door.

Stan is such a dick. I feel like going back into the bathroom and flushing the toilet. How can he make me feel like this? How can he make me feel so hot and good and then, on the turn of a dime, so alone and used? He could sure make me feel like a slut sometimes.

I seriously do not want to be inside my bedroom by the time he gets out of the shower. I do not care whether he is bare naked displaying his amazing body to me or fully dressed to the nines. I do not want to see him. I do not want to be anywhere near him. I am declaring that it is over between us. End the chapter please.

I am done. No more Stan. I have to promise myself that. It is time to find me a real man, not some teenage boy in a man's body.

Starting next week, I am going to free myself from Stan.

Right now, I am getting ahead of myself. I will have to wait and hide until Stan leaves my house.

Where can I hide where he will not be able to find me? Yes, of course. My basement!

I run down the stairs to my basement and hide in my laundry room. Then, about an hour later of hearing Stan hunting for me around my house, he left and slammed the front door.

I let out a sigh of relief. I can sleep well tonight.

Well, after I lock the front door, turn on my alarm system, clean up my kitchen, wipe up the vomit off the bathroom floor, pick up the wet towels, wipe down the shower doors, and clean up everything else that Stan made a mess of.

Yes, after all of this, I will be able to say that it will be a good night after all.

CHAPTER 13

I feel good. I feel recharged. I hardly saw Stan because he is busy with the new clients and the new mergers that he has no time to seduce me or harass me or hurt me again.

He is in meetings all day. I make sure he does not see me. I avoid him at all costs.

I am in my office sitting at my desk. I am still debating in my mind whether I should go to the police or not about what he had done to me.

I decide not to. I decide to plan for my job interview for Wednesday when there is a knock at my door. It is not Stan's knock, but then he could be drunk again. You just never know with people.

I look towards the door.

It is not Stan. It is a guy—a man. A really handsome man. Wow! He is incredible looking.

Perfect timing whoever you are. I am so happy. Finally, someone to distract me from Stan—the perfect specimen. Please tell me your name and I will tell you mine. Ask me for my phone number please. Ask me out to dinner! I will not say no like I say to Stan.

I stand up from my desk and walk around my desk to the door to greet this man. Whoever he is, he is tall and has a solid build. As I get closer to the door, I can see that his black blazer is unbuttoned and is wide open. I can see the outline of his abs through his tight-fitting black button-down shirt. His tight-fitting black pants to match showed his big muscular thighs.

When I am finally standing right in front of him, I can see that this man is incredibly handsome. He has black hair combed perfectly straight to one side, blue eyes, and a nice tan. He is clean-shaven with no hint of a beard or facial hair.

He is impeccably dressed in his three-piece black suit with a white handkerchief folded into a triangle sticking out of the front pocket of his jacket and black shoes to match. What a beautiful suit. He has an incredible smile with perfect white teeth.

"Hello. My name is Andrew Whitmore. I am so sorry to bother you, but I am lost. I have a meeting with Doug Harrison, but I do not know where his office is. Would you be so kind as to show me to Doug's office please?" His voice is lush.

Oh, my gosh! Is he trying to seduce me too? I cannot take it—two men at once. Who was I, Marilyn Monroe?

Really? What do I care? I will lead him anywhere he wanted to go except to the women's bathroom. I had already gone in there and it smelled terrible in there. Greta Stolz from accounting had stunk it up. I had no idea what she had for lunch, but she had better never eat whatever she ate ever again.

Andrew wanted to know where Doug's office was. Well, since I have so much work to do and there were about twenty other people in the office today that were available and that he could have asked them instead, I will be more than glad to show him around. He did not have to ask me twice.

Andrew is standing in front of me looking so dreamy. He is total eye candy and so worth the wait. I introduce myself. "Hi Andrew. My name is Mary Beth. I will be glad to show you to Doug's office. Right this way please."

Andrew moved to the side so I could walk by him to lead him to Doug's office. It is a big ass office. I am surprised that he does not have a kitchen and a bathroom in there.

I knock on Doug's door. It is open. "What do you want Mary Beth?" Doug said not bothering to look up.

"Geez, Doug. Good morning to you too. I have a client of yours here, Andrew Whitmore, who got lost and needed help getting to your office. He said he has an appointment with you." I motion for Andrew to walk into Doug's office.

Doug's mouth dropped open, and he started to stutter. I guess this guy is really important to the company. Who knew?

"It was nice meeting you, Mr. Andrew Whitmore. Maybe I will see you around." I started to walk away.

Andrew turned around inside the doorway and locked eyes with me. "Oh, I know you will. Until next time, Mary Beth. I do not forget a face." He smiled at me. His eyes were hypnotizing, mesmerizing just like Stan's were. We both stared at each other for a moment.

"Do you or do you not have work to catch up on, Mary Beth? Andrew and I have important business to discuss which has nothing to do with you. Please go back to your office now. Thank you. Your work here is finished," Doug said smugly.

Well, that was the last time I did something nice for Doug, but as for Andrew, I knew I would be dreaming of him tonight.

Andrew was looking at Doug, who was looking at me, and I was looking at Andrew. A very intense moment if I do not say so myself. I turned and walked away from Doug's office.

I could hear Andrew and Doug arguing as I was walking back to my office. Wow! The last time that someone yelled at Doug they were escorted out of the building or they were fired.

Anyway. I was sort of annoyed because Stan was not in his office to see me with Andrew walking down the hallway to Doug's office. I feel powerful this morning. I mean I feel powerful today. I enter my office and find to my surprise more piles of paperwork on my desk and a note from dear old Stan.

<u>Stan's note read:</u>

"Thank you so much for last night Mary Beth. You left me so hot and bothered. Have lots of fun doing my paperwork and remember to do it all with a smile. The same smile that I saw on your face last night. Wink."

Oh no. The two of us in the shower. Stan's hands on my body. Oh gosh. I turn beat red right then. I could feel my cheeks flush.

Oh, my gosh. Stan is a pervert. I walk over to my desk and pick up the paperwork. I turn around, walk out of my office and head right towards Stan's office.

I do not bother to knock. I am too pissed off. I burst open the door to Stan's office. I do not care if Stan is in his office. I do not care who is in Stan's office.

Stan was in his office sitting down at his desk on the phone talking to someone. He was facing away from the door.

When I reached his desk, he turned around in his chair. He must have heard me ruffling all of the papers. He smiled at me. He reached his hand out to me for me to take it but instead I slapped his hand away and I dropped the pile of paperwork right onto his lap.

The papers slid down his lap and onto the floor at his feet. He did not move to pick them up. He cocked his head up and to the side and opened his mouth just a little. A little *o* shape on his lips formed, and then he put his hand over the phone and looked at me.

Stan looked into my eyes that looked like razor blades and said, "This is not what I wanted to be placed on my lap you know." And with that he turned his chair back around so that he was facing away from me. He started talking again on the phone like nothing ever happened. Unbelievable.

I am furious. I want to throw something at the back of his head. He was not paying any attention to me anymore. I pick up a pen and almost stab him with it. I put the pen back down on his desk and walk out of his office extremely pissed off.

I walk out of Stan's office and run smack into Andrew.

My chest is pounding. It hurts so bad. And my shoulders are throbbing too. I cannot think straight. I feel dizzy.

Andrew could not have gotten lost again, could he? I am way too busy right now to give him my phone number or to have sex with him right now even though I really want to.

I am in shock. I am on the ground. My head really hurts now and so does the rest of my body. The pain slowly increases every minute that I try to sit up from the floor.

What did Andrew want now? To know the color of my underwear. Well, I might tell him. I think he can see my underwear because my skirt has ridden up my thighs a little bit.

To make matters worse, Stan witnessed our collision from his desk. Stan saw the spark between Andrew and I as we were trying to help each other up from the floor.

Stan saw the dance that Andrew and I were playing; the vibes between us, our vibrating chests and our heavy breathing—well, mine at least. I looked at Stan and from the look on Stan's face he did not look happy.

Andrew had just slammed right into me like a runaway locomotive. Andrew was not breathing heavy at all. Unbelievable.

Andrew started talking calmly to me, "I am so sorry Mary Beth for bumping into you. It was an accident I promise. Are you alright? I want to say it was on purpose, but no not really." He started to laugh.

"What? What do you mean?" I am so exasperated. I am trying to breathe. Now I am downright pissed off. How could Andrew laugh?

I pull down my skirt and I try to straighten myself out. I probably needed to take five Advil. I am in so much pain. Great another night at the hospital. I swear that I am setting some sort of record.

We both kneel down on the carpet to pick up the papers that were scattered on the floor.

Andrew was stuttering and muttering and trying to talk. I am trying hard to not look at him, but I feel his eyes on me. I could feel myself blushing. He is so good-looking. How could I stay mad at him?

Andrew started talking again. "What I meant was… what I meant to say is, that I wanted to bump into you again. I was hoping to bump into you again. I thought you were nice to help me find Doug's office. You are a nice person. I spoke to Doug. I told him I did not like the way that he spoke to you this morning and that he needs to treat you with more respect from now on."

Wow! I am in shock! I slowly stop picking up the papers off the floor and lift my head, absorbing the shock of what he had just said to me. I could only imagine how Doug must have reacted. He had probably laughed out loud and now would treat me even worse than he does now. Thank you, Andrew for making my life more miserable. I do not want to know what Doug will say to me the next time he sees me.

"Thank you, Andrew, for speaking up for me. I really appreciate it. You did not have to do that. That was truly kind of you. Doug does what Doug wants to do unfortunately."

Andrew stood up from the floor and gave me his hand and helped me up. Andrew was looking right into my eyes when he spoke, "Not anymore." He spoke with a calmness that had an edge to it that scared me.

And with that, he picked up the remaining papers from the floor and took the papers from my hands and walked away without looking back.

What happened between him and Doug? Did he make a complaint about Doug to someone? Oh no. My life is ruined.

I am so flustered that I had forgotten that I was standing right in front of Stan's office. I turned to look, and Stan's office door is still wide open. I can see him sitting in his chair at his desk. He is not talking on the phone anymore. He is staring at me. He is mad. The look on his face is purely possessive.

I have to get away fast.

Stan stood up from his chair and started to walk around his desk, but I just turned and ran as fast as I could back to my office, turned off the lights, and closed the door.

I hid underneath my desk. I am so hoping he will not bother me, and he did not. I saw him pass by my office door without stopping. Phew. That was a close one.

CHAPTER 14

The next day came and went without any kind of drama from anyone. The office for once was calm and peaceful. It was one the most normal days at work that I have had in a long time.

Doug decided to take the day off. Stan had to attend a meeting downtown all day long with Mr. Mark Greenland and all of the senior partners.

I finally had time to catch up on all of my emails and attend all of my meetings.

I decided to take a long lunch with Rebecca and then I decided to take a long walk around the city afterwards. Rebecca could not come along because she had to get back to the office. She told me to have fun but to behave myself.

I just took it easy all day on myself. It was like a vacation. It would not be this way for long, so I wanted to take advantage of it. I did some window shopping. I also bought myself some ice cream.

I swear I saw Stan through a window at a table with a lot of people at a restaurant when I was walking with Rebecca to lunch. I think that I am being paranoid. Stan and everyone are supposed to be across town. Oh, who cares!

Before I went back to the office, I stopped at a couple of my favorite clothing stores and I bought some new suits, new shoes, and new clothes.

I am feeling really happy by the time I get back to the office. I show Rebecca what I bought. We were laughing and joking for a little while before I headed upstairs to my office.

I cannot believe it. I am actually finished with all of my work for once, on time no less. My normal hours are usually 7am until 7pm give or take the workload.

I stand up from my desk and leave to go home.

I am in the lobby. I see Rebecca. I wave to her and say goodnight to her. She is about to leave herself. It is still daylight outside when I start to walk to my car. What a nice change for once.

I get to my house and take a nice hot shower first thing. While in the shower, I catch myself dreaming of Stan's hands touching me and Stan kissing my lips. Chills go up and down my body just thinking about Stan's touch and his kisses. I swear that I can almost hear Stan's voice say to me, "Mary Beth. Are you thinking of me? Do you need a hand?" Oh, my gosh. My face flushes. I have to get out of the shower now. I finish my shower quickly and head out of the bathroom.

After my much-needed shower, I dry myself off and blow-dry my hair and put on my skincare. I make my way downstairs in my pajamas, my bathrobe, and my slippers. I make myself a nice dinner and pour myself some wine.

I pull a small table in front of my couch in the living room. I place my food and my wine onto the table. I turn on the TV and I look at the clock on the DVR. It is only 8:30pm. I am so happy.

At 7:15am Wednesday morning, I am on the train to Massachusetts. I am sitting in a club car staring out the window. Seeing that life was passing me by, was this interview worth my time? Would it get any easier for me? Or maybe it would only get worse? I shuddered to think. I shake my head and try hard not to think about Stan and that night.

I dreamed about Stan the night he had left my house. I wondered if it meant, well, anything. Did he dream of me too?

I start to doze off. I dream of Stan. In my dream we are on a date and walk side by side with a small gap between us. Then suddenly, he closes the distance between us, and he gets closer to me and then he grabs my hand and squeezes it and gives me a smile. He stops walking and he pulls me close. He cups my chin in his hands and kisses me. Stan and those hypnotizing eyes—wow. I wonder if we will see each other again like that night. What will it be like the next time we are alone together?

Oh, shut up Mary Beth. Get your head out of the clouds and wake up!

By the time I exit the train and the terminal, it is 2:05pm. When I arrive, I have to find a cab. I still have to go over my questions for the interview and grab something to drink. I am so on edge. I have the hiccups. Maybe I should get something to eat as well. I see the cabs. Here goes nothing.

As I am heading back to New York on the 5:17pm train, in my head I am thinking I nailed it! I nailed the interview. I kicked ass. I smile. I am so proud of myself. I memorized all the questions that I wanted to ask them, and I was lucky to know how to answer all the questions the interviewers wanted to ask me.

Funny, isn't it, how this all worked out so well? I was the last person to board the train, but I got the best seat on the train. I am so lucky today. I guess it is a good start to a new beginning.

All of a sudden, I start to feel sad. I lower my head down and I start to silently cry to myself. I do not care about my mascara running or anything at this point. Maybe I have been holding back. Maybe I just need a good cry. I do not realize it at first but people on the train are staring at me. One older gentleman sitting across from me was kind and gave me some of his tissues.

The man said to me," Whatever your problems are now, they will be a thing of the past soon. Do not worry. Remember to smile." I am so surprised. The only thing that I could bring myself to say to him was, "Thank you. I hope so." I gave him a weak smile.

He smiled back at me one last time and went back to reading his newspaper.

I am blowing my nose and then I realize his tissues smelled like candy. It makes my stomach growl. I am hungry. I should have eaten before I left Massachusetts. I am too tired to get up now and go to the food car. So, I sit in silence for the remainder of the trip.

I finally get off the train. It was late, almost 10:30pm. Oh, my gosh. I totally forgot that I have to go to work tomorrow. I thought that it was Saturday, but it is only Wednesday. Didn't I say that I was taking off Thursday and Friday? Oh no. I must have forgotten to. Oh well.

I am walking back to my car from the train station when I start to feel this all-too-familiar feeling inside my stomach. I can see a figure in the dark appear as I approach my car. I cannot make out the face. Do I know this person? Is this person a figment of my imagination? I cannot look away, but I still cannot believe someone is leaning up against my car.

It all appears so clear to me as to who it is.

It is Stan Howler. What is he doing here? What does he want?

I am close enough to my car to hear Stan say to me with such anger in his voice, "Why did you do it Mary Beth? How dare you? You did not have to do this. I told you that you did not have to leave me. You can stay here with me. I said that I will take care of you. I do not want you to leave me. It does not have to be this way and you know it."

"Too late, Stan. My mind is made up. You made it up for me. You cannot hurt me anymore." Just like that. I feel so good talking back to Stan. I will not allow him to hurt me anymore. I finally found my voice and my inner strength to speak up for myself.

"This is my life, Stan. You have no say. Back away from my car. How dare you stalk me? I might just go to the police station on my way home. See you tomorrow at work. Good night."

As I said these words to him, he did in fact back away from my car. He was totally shocked that I had spoken to him like that.

I am in a really grouchy mood and I do not care at all. I unlock my car, open the car door, climb in, slam the car door on him, and drive away without even looking in the mirror.

Home sounded great. I will have a glass of wine, a nice bubble bath, and a nice home-cooked meal. It all sounds fabulous, and I am worth it. I do not care what time it was.

Good for you. You told Stan who's boss. You go, girl. He will not wreck my life like before. No way. Not now.

I turn on my car radio and Aretha Franklin's "Respect" is playing. That is right Stan, you give me the respect that I deserve.

I get home, turn on the lights, and take off my coat and put it on one of my kitchen chairs. I make sure this time that no one has followed me, and I remember to lock my front door and to look outside my windows. I turn on my alarm system. You can never be too careful anymore these days.

I really hope the Massachusetts firm likes me enough to offer me the position. I really liked it there. I had felt a real connection. It is not like my present job, where I feel so disconnected from everyone and where my co-workers and my bosses take me for granted.

Where is my wine? I needed a glass of wine badly. I had bought everything at the grocery stores before I left for Massachusetts. I am standing here in the middle of my kitchen totally worn out. I sigh.

I let out this huge scream in the middle of my kitchen. I feel so much better now. Letting out steam is always good now and then. I hope no one heard me scream and decided to call the police. I stopped to listen for any sirens. None. Thank gosh.

I turn around and make it up the stairs to my bedroom doorway. I am hesitant to enter my bedroom. It is dark. I wait and I listen outside my bedroom door. Nothing out of the ordinary. Phew.

I walk into my bedroom and I turn on the light. I realize there is nothing to worry about so, I go about my business.

I still am not 100 percent trusting myself just, yet I guess. I put my purse on my dresser. I change into my pajamas, robe, and my slippers and make my way downstairs to the kitchen.

I pour myself a glass of wine. I take out the utensils and plates that I am going to need for my dinner. I decide to make myself a sandwich. I want to watch some TV before I go to bed tonight.

I go and turn the light on in my living room. I turn on the TV and flip through the channels. I stop at the channel playing *Modern Family*. I love this show. I cannot remember the last time I had the chance to sit down and enjoy this show. It is heaven.

I sit on my sofa and get comfortable and watch TV and laugh. This feels so unnatural, but it feels so good. I have to do this more often.

I pause the show and make it back into the kitchen. I am so hungry. I need more food. I make myself another sandwich and then walk back to the fridge for some veggies and pour myself some ranch dressing.

I go back into the fridge and get some oranges out and begin cutting them. They taste so good. The juice drips down my chin and onto my pajama shirt. It is 11:45pm on a work night and I do not care. I do not have a care in the world.

The night got away from me. It was a mix of drinking wine and eating really good food. My dessert of choice is a tiramisu cake—so good. I ate so much and laughed so loud while watching *Modern Family.*

It was about 1:00am when I finished eating and watching TV. I put all of my dishes into the sink. I can do the dishes tomorrow. I slowly make it up the stairs. I am so tired. I take off of my bathrobe and drop it on the floor. I plop into my bed and fall asleep without using the bathroom. Wow. Life hit me hard today—until tomorrow. What did tomorrow have in store for me? Did I dare to find out?

Little did I know that Stan was watching me the whole time through my kitchen windows while I was having a blast pigging out and laughing so hard at the TV.

CHAPTER 15

Boy, did I overdo it last night or what? I am so incredibly late for work. I did not wake up until 11:00am. I thought that I was dreaming.

I looked at my alarm clock and said, "Holy Potatoes!"

I have to get my myself together and get to work or I would not have a job. Somehow, I cleaned up nice and fast and made it to work without anyone—and I mean anyone—noticing or saying anything to me. I think everyone thought that I slept here most every night, so maybe they thought that I was out to lunch. I mean, mentally I really am.

I am so hungover, and I am so tired, but I feel that I can definitely keep it together if Doug and Stan decide to make a surprise visit to my office. And wouldn't you know it, they do. Thank gosh I had makeup on, and I had brushed my teeth.

A few minutes later I hear, "Well, well, what do we have here? We have our best employee hard at work. Doesn't she look like she's going to throw up Stan?"

That could only mean one thing. Doug. I pick my head up from my desk as soon as I hear his voice. I cringe. Doug. One word—yuck!

"Well, Mary Beth, we've just signed a contract with a new partner. A new firm will be merging with us, and we'll be making an obscene amount of money. We just want to ask you if you want to come out tonight and celebrate with us— you know, have a few drinks at the local bar around the corner. I'll be buying," said Doug with a nice big smile on his face.

Yeah right. Doug paying. That is a joke. Stan has to pay for everything, always. When did Doug ever pay for anything? I am so hungover. I just want to go home and vomit, but lucky me Stan always could persuade me.

"Well, Mary Beth, what do you say? Say yes." Stan said to me, looking at me with his goofy grin and that smile. I cannot tell if it was a smirk or something else. My vision is quite blurry. "Sure, why not?" I say without trying to sound hungover.

Stupid Mary Beth. You need to go home after work and make yourself a Bloody Mary or something. Have some coffee. Not go out for drinks with dumb and dumber.

"We will come back to pick you up sometime after 5:00pm," Doug said to me and then they both walked away.

I could see the happiness in their eyes and the dollar signs. It is always about the money.

I could see them both walking down the hallway side by side. They gave each other pats on each other's back, and they both were grinning from ear to ear. They exchanged high fives back and forth until I could not see them anymore.

I get up and go to the bathroom and throw up. I feel that Doug and Stan were making feel sick or maybe it was just Stan in general. Maybe it was the wine. It probably was all of the above.

I got out of the bathroom. Thank gosh no one came in. I barely make it to the break room. I make tea for myself with milk and sugar—lots of sugar. I need to wake up. I feel so tired.

I head back to my desk after a few sips of tea and finding a much-needed bagel, cream cheese, and some fruit in the break room.

When I get back to my office, I find all the piles of work that Stan and Doug had stacked onto my desk for days has vanished. Am I hallucinating?

Well, half of it is gone at least, unless they are trying to pull a prank on me.

I sure hope they have found another sucker to do the work. Maybe I am too good. Or maybe I am too slow. It does not matter. It is no longer my responsibility. Goodbye to the both of them and to all of the paperwork.

I barely make it through the day. A couple more trips to the bathroom, more food and coffee help me from feeling so nauseous. I need water badly. I feel so dehydrated.

As the time goes by, I have to go to the bathroom a few more times and then the clock on my office wall chimes. It is 5:00pm on the dot. Wow. Time has gone by so quickly. I still feel so sick. I think maybe I will take a rain check.

I look out of my office door and peek down the hallway. I do not see anyone. I think that I can slip out with anyone knowing that I have left for the day. I am struggling to put on my coat. Oh, what am I thinking? Who is waiting for me at 5:08pm in my office doorway and calling me sweet cheeks? None other than Stan.

"Are you ready yet, sweet cheeks? How come you are not ready yet? Oh, come on. Hurry up Mary Beth." Stan walked into my office and helped me into my coat. "Oh Mary Beth. Don't you know that it is time to go? I want to get going. I have to make sure that you come out with us. It is especially important that you be there. Hurry up and get your things. I am waiting. People are waiting. I want to make sure that Doug does not drink all the good wine. Lush that he is," Stan's tone was bitter.

What was on his mind?

I slowly start to button my coat and put things into my purse. Of course, I am moving too slowly because Stan is watching me and his facial expression changes to concern. Gee, that is a first. I hold up my hand to him to make him stop advancing towards me.

"Stop right there Stan. I am fine. I am tired. You do not have to wait for me or escort me to the bar. I will be right there. I know where the bar is." I said this with as much courage as I could muster. What I really wanted to do was make my way over to Stan and punch his lights out for making me feel so miserable. I blame Stan and Doug for making me drink so much last night. I have been feeling so stressed out lately. Gee I wonder why?

Stan left a minute later. I do not care if I have hurt his feelings or that I pissed him off. I am at my limit.

I pick up my purse from my desk and close it. I start to walk slowly out the door when, suddenly, my feet give way. I start to fall to the floor, but then I feel strong hands tighten around my waist and back.

Oh no. It is Stan. I am sure he is loving this moment. He will never allow me to forget it. He will hold this over my head every time he needs a favor or wants to upset me.

Remember the time you needed my help and I helped you, Mary Beth. I can only hear him now.

Stan can look at me all he wants to, but I do not want him to touch me anymore—not ever.

"Are you all right, Mary Beth? I am concerned about you. Are you sick? Can I take you to the hospital? Do you need medical attention?" Stan said this without hesitation or judgment. He truly is concerned. Wow!

Stan really did have a heart, just not for me. His heart is reserved for everyone else except me of course. Silly me. I am daydreaming. Here we are—me and Stan, Stan and me, in the hallway right outside my office, just the two of us in each other's arms. He is holding me, and I am holding onto him. I think to myself, never again. This can never happen again.

I am having feelings of revulsion and disgust for him. He makes me feel sick. I want to puke all over him. I cannot believe that it takes this much for him to care about me. He has been such a terrible friend to me. He has been taking advantage of me for such a long time.

I am happy to know, thank gosh, that the others have already made their way to the bar, so they cannot see what is going on between me and Stan right now.

Everyone would have seen right through me right then and there. I try so hard not to give in and look at him. I close my eyes and tense up. Stan felt me tense up.

"What is wrong with you Mary Beth? Why are you acting this way?" Stan said to me.

I can feel his eyes looking right through me. He wants to know the truth. I do not want to tell him. I do not want him to know, but when you are drunk you spill the beans. So here goes. Mind you, when you are drunk and hung-over, you cannot take back what you say ever. Maybe it is a mistake. Maybe it is not.

"Stan, I am so drunk over you. I think you know this." And as I said this, I pass out in his arms.

When I wake up, I do not know where I am. It all looks so familiar, but I cannot place it.

Oh no. Oh, my gosh. I wake up in horror. I am in Stan's office. I am laying down on Stan's couch with my head in his lap. Oh no, someone call the cops. He took advantage of me. I just know it. Is my coat undone, my blouse unbuttoned, and is my skirt unzipped? I have a bad headache, and it hurts to sit up, but I try to sit up regardless.

A familiar soft voice soothes my nerves. "Calm down. It is just me Mary Beth do not get overly excited. You are in my office. Lay down. Do not move. Here, take some Advil and drink some water." I just stare at him, but I do not move.

"Mary Beth please take it. Do not look at me like that. I am here for you Mary Beth. I want to help you. I can at least try, can't I? Stan starts to laugh. Do not worry Mary Beth I did not take advantage of you. I just carried you in my arms here into my office when you passed out. I am concerned about you. You scared me. I thought that I had to call an ambulance for you."

"Thank you, Stan for everything and for not taking advantage of me. I am a mess. Everything with me is a mess. I do not deserve your kindness. I do not deserve this. I do not want it either. Just go away and leave me alone. I am so shocked that you did not take advantage of me," I said.

Stan is upset. He said to me, "Do not say those words to me Mary Beth. That is foolish. What I have come to realize these last few days is that I feel that *I am* not the one to deserve your kindness. I have taken advantage of you every step of the way. I played games with you. I realize that I wanted to, and I still want to play games with you. To be honest I like it… all of it…until now of course, given this very moment. You are sick Mary Beth, and you need someone to take care of you. I want to be the one. I would like it to be me. I know that I screwed up and you know that I cannot give you all of me right now. I do not want to do this anymore. This back and forth between you and me. I feel that it is too much—too much tension, too much animosity, too much anxiety. I can help you out with whatever you need help with, except certain things. I will not push you again like that. I hurt you and I am sorry. It has taken a while for me to realize this. When you fell into in my arms in the hallway outside of your office not too long ago, I could have had my way with you. I would have liked that very much, ever since the other night that we were together, but then, you did not move or talk and then you were not breathing, and I got scared. Say something please, Mary Beth—anything. Say that you forgive me. Please."

"Time to make the donuts. There I said something." Clunk. I started to close my eyes but not before I saw Stan smile and I could hear him start to laugh at me.

Stan sat back on the sofa and looked at me and smiled. He shook his head and laughed some more at my expense. He really laughed hard. It is so good to hear his laugh, and so I try to smile too, but it hurts to smile. It hurts to feel anything. It just hurts too darn much. Then I passed out… again.

CHAPTER 16

When I wake up, Stan is nowhere to be found. It is dark and quiet in his office. I can hear the air coming through the vents. I can hear a clock ticking. I can even hear my own heartbeat.

"Figures. So much for I want to take care of you Mary Beth. Where are you now Stan? I need a drink. Where do you keep your liquor, Stan?" I said.

No, no, no, Mary Beth wrong answer.

Oh right, I need water or juice and pretzels and maybe some Ginger Ale. That is what I really need right now. Not alcohol. I am still weak, but I remember the many times being in here—in Stan's office. I know that he has a fridge in here somewhere. I will probably bash my knees or a body part on something before I find it. I am struggling to stand up from the couch.

I remember the fridge being in the corner to my left the last time I was in here, so maybe I do not need the lights.

Bam! I crash into what seems like a table with chairs. I hear something like a glass or a cup with liquid in it tip over and then I think there were folders with papers in them fly off the table. I cannot have been more wrong. I trip on something and fall to the carpet and the next thing that I know I feel something wet on my elbows. Water or coffee. Oh, no. Oh, crap. Stan will be so pissed at me if I got his papers wet. I need to hightail it out of here before he comes back.

Man did that hurt. I am going to have a million bruises all over my body. I know it. I will look at my body when I get home if I could get home. I have no idea what time it is. It is probably midnight or later. I struggle to get up from the floor. I have to use the table to help me up.

Stan is such a sick person that he probably has cameras in his office and is watching me right now on his TV at his home or on his cellphone, laughing at me and then he will go and show Doug. Probably tomorrow he will tell me all about it. He will want to show me so he can tell me what a fool I have been.

Great. I cannot wait. I am so glad that he found me so entertaining sometimes. Sometimes I just could not stand him. He can be such a jerk sometimes and a rotten friend as well.

I have to admit that he has been nice to me for like fifteen seconds tonight. That should count for something, right? No. It did not make up for all of the horrible ways that he has treated me thus far.

I want to go home. I want to forget about Stan and him holding me in his arms. When I woke up and saw the way that he was looking at me on his sofa— that face, those eyes. I close my eyes and my whole-body shakes with fear. I do not want to remember. If only I could click my heels three times and wake up and be somewhere nice like Turks and Caicos. That would be fantastic.

I am so exhausted. I crawl my way back to the sofa. I feel around the office to get to the door. I feel for the lights and turn them on. I look for my keys and my purse. They are on the sofa and my coat is on the back of Stan's desk chair. I make it out of Stan's office very slowly without crashing into anything else, thank gosh. Stan not only turned out the lights to his office, but he had closed his office door and locked it. Unbelievable.

Could I just have one normal day to myself without having any drama? Is this in any way possible?

I finally make it down to the front desk and pass the security guard on my way out, and he said good night to me. I still have no idea what time it is. I do not know why I care so much.

I am walking to my car. I hope no one will jump out and scare me. I think of Stan and how he stalked me all the way to my house the other night and made his way into my house without even knocking, without even caring. He could be so selfish sometimes. What had I ever seen in him?

I start to think back about everything that has happened with Stan. It is too late to make any changes now. All of my tears, heartache, pain, energy, and my time were all wasted on a self-absorbed man.

All the time and energy that I spent thinking of him, crying over him, drooling over him, making a fuss about him and making him fit into my life—it was all gone. It is never coming back. I will never get any of it back no matter how hard

I try. I start to cry. I stop walking and put my head into my hands. I did this a lot lately. I have to stop doing this to myself. Where is Dr. Phil when you need him?

I want to go on vacation to the Turks and Caicos. Just me. That sounds great. I pick up my head from my hands and start to walk again to my car. Darn it all. I do not think that I have the money though.

I could ask Stan for a loan or a raise maybe. Knowing Stan, the way that I do know him, he would probably flip out and not give it to me and then make me take him to Turks and Caicos with me. Then I would have to entertain him for the duration of my stay there. Nope. Not a good idea. Not going to happen. Bad idea.

I finally get to my car. I am so sleepy. I hope I will not fall asleep while I am driving home. I unlock my car, open my driver's side door, put on my safety belt and then start my car.

I pull out into the dark night that I felt was swallowing me whole. I start driving towards my house, but someone is following me.

CHAPTER 17

I am driving my car, like usual, but I feel something is off. It is not because I am drunk or hungover. I feel something else. I cannot figure out what it is, but the feelings that I am having are really scaring me. It is like something bad is going to happen to me, but I have no idea what. It is out of my control.

I am sitting at a red light waiting for the light to turn green. I am not far from my house. Why is the light not turning green? It seems like minutes have gone by without the light changing. To the right of me is a one-way street that you cannot go down and then I see a car parked to the side on the street and there appears to be some sort of light inside the car. Maybe a cellphone or a computer and then I turn away from the light in the car because I see headlights starting to appear in my rearview mirror. Then a dark SUV appears.

It is late at night and I start to look out the windows of my car and see that there is no one around. My neighborhood is so quiet. Shoot. No one will see anything if something happens to me out here. I do not think that the town has fixed the traffic cameras yet. They have been down for a week now.

I see the dark SUV getting closer to my car, but then at about 10 feet away from my car the dark SUV just suddenly disappears. I do not see any headlights anymore. It is hard to see the SUV without turning around in my seat and having my seat belt cut into my neck.

I fully turn around in my seat and I am looking for the SUV. I see headlights turn on and they blind me. They are so bright. I have to put my hands over my eyes. I hear a car engine roar.

Oh no.

I turn around in my seat as quickly as I possibly can. I can see from the right side of my car that the SUV was heading right towards me at full speed. The SUV almost slammed right into me. I am able to get out of the way just in the nick of time to avoid being hit. Thank gosh there were no other cars around when the car accident happened.

I feel that I hit my head on the steering wheel as my car went up on the curb and crashed into something. I think that I am bleeding.

I pick my head up. I think I am looking at some garbage cans. Oh wait. Are you kidding me? After tonight I still have to put out the garbage! You have to be kidding me!

I forgot that it is garbage day. Now I have to put out the garbage. Really? After all this? This day is just terrible.

I put my head down on the steering wheel but to the side, looking out the window to my left. My head really hurt. I could see from the side mirror that someone is getting out of the SUV.

I did not hear or see the SUV pull up behind me. I hear a car door slam. I hear footsteps start to approach my driver side door. I am waiting to hear the gun shot. Oh gosh. I hope that my underwear is clean. I could only hear my mom now.

"You know officer, my daughter never wore clean underwear as a child, and I told her to put clean underwear on all the time. But no, she would not listen to me. Now look at her. I am so disappointed in her, but at least her hair looks good. She always had nice hair."

The person is only 5 feet away now from my car and then a light from a house comes on.

Then, I see another light come on and then another. Doors started to open up and people start to come outside and look around. Whoever it is, turns around, gets back into their car and speeds away.

What a crazy person! What the ——! Holy Crap! What just happened? I am not okay. I am shaken up. I am out of my mind. Where is a cop when you need one? Not a cop in sight. Gee, lucky me.

Cops are never around when you need one. I cannot believe this—at this time of night. What are the chances? Why doesn't one of my neighbors pick up the phone and call 9-1-1?

I finally calm down and could breathe normally. I struggle to find my purse to get my cellphone out and dial 9-1-1. I guess that I have to do it myself.

I tell the dispatcher what happened, and amid the nightmare that has just occurred, the person got close enough to my car so that I could get a partial on the SUV's license plate.

What a dumbass! The person should be arrested and put in jail for life! I could have a concussion. My head is throbbing, and I definitely taste blood.

The dispatcher said a police officer would be there shortly and asked me if I was injured and if I needed medical attention. I said yes, I need medical attention please. Then the dispatcher told me to breathe and to stay calm. The dispatcher asked what happened and what was wrong with me. The dispatcher said that they would stay on the phone with me until the ambulance and the police arrived.

I wait and wait and wait. All of the people that had come out of their houses are just standing on their porches staring at me. Not one of them came over to check on me to see if I am ok. What horrible neighbors I have.

Finally, I see the lights and I hear the sirens of the police and the ambulance. I breathe a sigh of relief. I said thank you and goodbye to the dispatcher. I hang up the phone.

The police officer is nice to me. He helps me out of my car and grabs my purse for me. He asks me if I am ok and then he helps me into the ambulance. He takes my statement while I am being taken care of.

I tell the police officer named Justin Forrester what happened. I give him the partial license plate number. I also tell him it was a Massachusetts license plate. I am too tired to think. I did not get a good look at the driver. I could not even tell what make or model the SUV was. It is a dark SUV. That is all I know.

What an ending to a new beginning I kept thinking to myself. I ended up with a big bruise/bump on my forehead, a split lip, a cut on my cheek, and a sprained wrist. No concussion. That was music to my ears. My air bag did not go off.

What a night! Can I go to bed yet? I am at the end of my rope, seriously. How long would I have to wait to go home, get into my pajamas, brush my teeth, and go to bed?

It is feeling like an eternity. It seems like I will never get out of the ambulance and get back to my car. Finally!

Justin, the nice police officer, insists on following me back to my house just to be safe. I park my car in my driveway and then I lock my car.

Justin parks his patrol car behind me in my driveway and gets out. He locks his car and then follows me up the driveway to my front door. He insists on helping me inside and to make sure my house is safe. He stays for a cup of coffee but no donuts. I do not have any donuts in my house to give him even if he had asked me for them.

We both sit at my kitchen table and he tells me that he was on his way back to the police station because his shift had ended, but then he got the call on the radio and said that he would take the call. I am glad that he did. He is genuinely concerned for me and is very patient with me. He told me that he had just gotten married a year ago and that he had a baby and she was just a few months old, and he and his wife named their baby girl Joyce.

Justin and I talked for a few more minutes and then he said that he has to leave. He tells me that another police officer would be here shortly to take over. His radio went off.

Justin got up from the kitchen table. I get up slowly and walk to the front door. I open the door for him.

Justin said, "Good night Mary Beth. Here is my card. If you remember anything else, please do not hesitate to give me a call. Take care of yourself. Have a good night." Justin walks out the door and walks to his car.

I close the door and lock it after I watch Justin walk back to his patrol car. I can see the other police cars pull up as Officer Justin is about to drive away. They were talking for a while and then Officer Justin drove away. I watch the police officers from my front windows.

I put my alarm system on and go back into my kitchen.

I take my coat off and place it on one of my kitchen chairs.

I walk over to my fridge. I am about to open the fridge door. I hear a very loud noise that makes me scream. I turn to hear where the noise is coming from. I walk over to the kitchen windows. There stood a person who had just thrown a rock at my kitchen windows. The person waved at me and then just stared at me. I am so terrified. The person outside is just as baffled as to why the glass did not break.

Well, it seems so because the person repeatedly tries to break the windows.

Who is this person? Do I know this person?

I realize now why the glass did not break. I remember that I invested a bunch of money into shatter-proof glass when I bought this house. My neighbor told me to get it. He said that there had been a lot of break-ins a few months back, so it was worth investing in.

I take a deep breath. I hear sirens coming closer to my house now and I feel safe again. I walk closer to the kitchen windows to see the person walk, not run, back towards his car.

Oh, my gosh! I could see through the kitchen windows that it looked like the same dark SUV that had tried to run me off the road earlier tonight. Justin, the police officer told me that the driver of this SUV had been reported before for doing the same thing by two other people.

Suddenly, I am frightened by a loud knock on my door and the lights flashing through my windows. I want to make sure it is a cop before I open my door.

I open my door to find two police officers. "Good evening," the police officers said. "We are the neighborhood police. My name is Officer Tom Reese, and this here is my partner Officer Bob Hardy. I heard the call on the radio. Given the earlier circumstances, we just wanted to check up on you. We got a call about a person looking suspicious outside. Did you see anything? Did you hear anything? Could you tell us what happened here tonight?"

"Yes, Officer Tom," I said. "The piece of crap person who tried to run me off the road earlier tonight is the same person who just now threw rocks at my kitchen window several times in order to break my windows. The person just waved and stared at me through the windows before continuing to throw several more rocks at my kitchen windows—until the person took off. I watched whoever it is get into what looks like the same SUV that was used in the attempted attack on me tonight. What is going on? I am really scared. I just want to go to sleep. I have had such a long bad day."

"I am sorry for what happened to you. May we come in and take a look around especially at your kitchen windows. We want to make sure that you are safe." Officer Tom Reese is really nice and understanding.

Both officers walk into my house and I close my front door. They both walk into my kitchen to check out my windows and then they made their rounds around my house until they came back to the front door where I am still standing.

Officer Bob Hardy said to me, "The windows in your kitchen seem to be intact. They are not broken. You should be fine. We did not find any broken locks or doors around your house. Our investigation into your case may take some time, but we hope to catch the person who is bothering you. We will call you if we get any leads. Take our cards. I hope you can get some rest now. Please call us if anything else happens. We will stay here outside your house for a while to see if the person comes back. Have a good night and lock your doors after we leave. Thank you."

"I will. I hope nothing else happens to me tonight." "Thank you, officers. Have a good night," I said.

"You are welcome," they both said to me as they walked back to their police cars.

Oh boy. What the freak! I cannot believe this is happening to me.

Can I please just get some sleep? Apparently not.

I close the front door and lock it. I put the alarm system on. I walk up the stairs to my bedroom. I change into my pajamas, brush my teeth and get into bed. I try to get some sleep, but I cannot sleep. I am too terrified.

I hear a noise. Oh, my gosh. What is it now? Is this person in my house? Oh no. How did they get in? I am being paranoid.

I listen and stay still. I listen for a long time. I sit up in my bed and listen some more. It sounds like someone is on my roof. What?

Man am I tired! I have to go to work tomorrow. I am going to be sleeping at my desk for sure. No coffee or tea is going to help me stay awake this time.

I get out of bed and walk over to one of my bedroom windows and open it. I look out to my right. The same two police officers are still there. Thank gosh. Then I look to my left, and I see it!

I see a person climbing up onto my roof with my own ladder! Oh, my gosh! I am not crazy. I am not hearing things. I can see from a distance from my bedroom window with the help of the streetlight… there is the dark SUV!

I ran so fast out of my bedroom and down the stairs. I opened the door to the world to see me without even thinking. Here I am in my scooby doo pajamas, my bunny slippers and my bathrobe. Talk about embarrassing myself.

Leaving the door wide open, I run to the police officers as fast as I can, screaming at the top of my lungs.

I scream all the way to them. Officer Tom steps out of his police car.

He grabs me by the shoulders and said, "What's the matter? Why are you screaming? Calm down. You have to calm down. Tell me what happened." He let go of my shoulders.

"The person, the person…" I am freezing cold. I am shivering. I cannot talk. It takes me a while to talk. "The person who has been terrorizing me tonight is trying to climb up to my roof and trying to get into my house right now. I just saw the person outside my bedroom window. Whoever it is, is wearing dark clothing."

"What? Are you sure? We have been doing checks all over your house," said Officer Bob.

"Yes," I said. "I know what I saw."

"Okay. We will do a perimeter check right now. Go back inside your house and lock your door," said Officer Bob.

I hear Officer Tom say into his radio that back up is needed and so is a helicopter before I run so fast back into my house. It is freezing cold outside.

I run inside my house, slam the door shut and lock the door. I walk over to the kitchen windows. There are some markings on the windows but thank gosh there are no cracks. I run my finger over the markings.

I am going to stay down here in my living room and lay down on the sofa and wait for the officers to knock on my door. I do not want to sleep. I am a crazy person trapped inside my own home.

What a terrifying situation. Who is doing this to me? Who would go to all this trouble to terrorize me like this? This is insane. I am terrified, but at the same time, exhausted. I cannot stay awake. I close my eyes, but I keep waking up repeatedly.

Finally, after what seemed like forever, there is a knock at my front door. It is Officer Tom, and he tells me the good news.

"Mary Beth. You do not have to worry anymore tonight. We caught the person who has been bothering you. He was drilling a hole into one of your solar paneled windows. We can call to have someone come and fix your windows sometime tomorrow. We will need to take your statement down at the station, but we can do that sometime tomorrow. Get some rest. Have a good night."

"Thank you, Officer Tom. And tell Officer Bob and the other police officers thank you as well. I am so appreciative of your assistance. I am so sorry that I am crying. I just feel so scared."

"It's okay. You are safe now. Take some deep breathes. We will be in contact with you tomorrow. Take care. Good night." Officer Tom offered me a smile and walked away.

I stare out into the night before I close my front door. I want so badly to see this guy who has been terrorizing me tonight. I see two different police officers drag the guy over to the police car, force him up against the police car, handcuff him and then place him into the cop car and slam the door. I could not see the person's face.

Darn it all. I want to know who it is.

The lights and sirens are blaring throughout the whole neighborhood. People are coming out of their homes in their pajamas and bathrobes by the dozens now. I can hear my neighbors shouting to the police. I finally decide to close my front door and go to bed. I lock the door and turn my alarm system on.

The phone rings and I get to talk to a nice security agent named Jake Scooter. I tell him that everything is alright, and that the police apprehended the suspect, and I am safe now.

An hour and a half later I am finally done talking to Jake.

Who would have thought that this whole scenario would happen to me? Why me? What have I done?

I feel so relieved though that the cops came to save me. What would have happened to me if they were not here to save me? I shudder to think.

CHAPTER 18

What time is it? Bed, Mary Beth. Who cares what time it is?

When I reach my bedroom, I walk straight over to my bed. The clock reads 2:18am on my nightstand. I fall on top of my covers and I pass out as soon as my head hits the pillow.

I wake up to sounds of people bustling about outside my window from the street. I cannot believe that it is morning already. I shudder to look at the clock. I cannot hide from it anymore.

It is 5:50am. Thank gosh. I can sleep for a little while longer and then I can take a shower and eat a good breakfast. I fall back to sleep. I finally get out of bed at 6:15am.

I take my time taking a shower and then getting dressed. I forget to look in the mirror at my face. I hardly put on any makeup. Why do my lips hurt so much?

I make it to the police station before going into work. It went well. They took my statement. They are still investigating my case and will contact me when they find out more information.

I thought driving to work would be scary, but there were no problems. I park my car and walk into work. No problems. No one is staring at me. No one is whispering. I am surprised that no one has heard about what happened to me last night. I am sure it will be all over the news tonight though.

Me! On the news! Oh no! Not what I want now.

Right now, I want my life to be normal. I want to do my work and then go home. I am scared to go home. There is a hole in my roof. What if it rains before my roof is fixed?

The day went by in the blink of an eye.

Stan said hi to me and was nice to me throughout the day. He did not mention last night at any time that we engaged in conversation. I am quite happy that he did not. I am in no shape to argue with him.

Stan came into my office and sat down on one of my office chairs in front of my desk near the end of the day. Stan talked to me for a long time, and he made me smile. He teased me about a lot of things. I liked the attention that he was giving to me.

Before I knew it, it was time to go home. I am petrified. Now would be a great time for Stan and Doug to put mountains of paperwork on my desk or ask me to go for a drink at the bar down the street.

Stan finally stood up and asked me, "Are you hungry? Do you want to grab some dinner with me?"

"Huh? What did you say? Sorry. I was not paying attention."

"I said, do you want to grab some dinner with me Mary Beth? Nothing fancy. My treat. Please say yes. Don't make me beg." Stan was grinning.

Given what happened to me last night, I am certainly not going to be going home to an empty house where there could be danger.

I said, "Sure. Sounds great."

"Good. I am so happy that you said yes and that I do not have to break your arm," Stan said to me.

I said, "Stan, what did you just say?" Stan said, "Nothing Mary Beth. Let me grab my coat and I will meet you back here in your office in 20 minutes. Is that enough time for you to get ready to leave?"

I said, "Yes. That is enough time for me to get ready to leave. That will be fine. See you back here in my office in 20 minutes." I smile at Stan. I am so glad that he asked me to go to dinner with him. I breathe a sigh of relief. I am so glad that I do not have to go home right away.

Wait a minute! What did Stan mean that he would break my arm? You don't think. No. Stan is not the type of person to hurt people. No, he could not be. What a silly idea to cross my mind. Wait, is Stan really capable of hurting me? Stan came back into my office before I could think any more about him and his capabilities.

We decided to go to dinner at a little Italian place called Little Italy right near our office. We had a good time together. We laughed and joked. I realized how much I missed hanging out with Stan as a friend. I smiled a lot—which was good under the given circumstances and the situations that have been thrown at me lately. One thing is for sure is that I definitely need to take better care of myself from now on.

Stan paid the bill just like he said he would. He walked me to my car. This time, I did not slam my car door in his face. He was appreciative of that. I turned the car on and rolled the window all the way down.

Stan rested his arms on my door and leaned in and said to me, "Thank you for not slamming your car door in my face like the last time. Last time I did, however, deserve it. I had fun tonight. I enjoyed myself. I hope you had a good time." He smiled at me.

I said, "Yes. I did have a good time. Thank you, Stan." I smiled back at him.

Stan and I lingered in the moment and in each other's company. We stared at each other for a while. Neither of us said anything. A few minutes later, he leaned in my window and put his face close to mine. He slowly cupped my face with his hands and kissed me ever so gently for the longest time on my lips and then Stan released me.

"If you must go my dear, Mary Beth, I will understand. It is complicated between us. I know. I have behaved badly. I understand if you want to leave. Remember, you will always have a friend in me, always. Never forget that." He blew me a kiss. "Good night, Mary Beth." And with that, he turned around and walked away into the night.

Is this the way we say goodbye to each other? I have to wonder. What is going on? What is Stan up to? I am so confused right now.

I watch Stan walk back to his car. I watch Stan drive away.

I leave the car window down and let the night's wind sweep over my face and into my hair while I am driving home.

I have so much to think about—about Stan, about my roof, and what about this job? What did Stan want? Is he playing tricks on me again? I do not know for sure, but I want to find out.

I hate secrets. I hate them. I hate surprises as well.

What did clever Stan have up his sleeve? I wonder. Did he really mean what he said before? Was he being sincere? For my sake, I sure hope so.

I get to my house and park my car in my driveway. I lock my car. I unlock my front door and close it shut. I lock my front door and turn on my alarm system. I am so exhausted. I am going to bed.

Wow! What a horrible week it has been so far except for maybe tonight.

Tomorrow is Friday. Thank gosh! What might happen to me tomorrow, though? I do not wish to think about tomorrow. I do not want to worry about what bad things might happen to me anymore.

To bed you go, Mary Beth. Do not pass go and do not collect $200—just go straight to bed.

Bed did sound good. I need a good night's rest.

CHAPTER 19

It is Friday morning. I wake up way before my alarm clock went off. I lay awake in the dark, my head is on my pillow. No TV and no radio. Not yet.

I am just thinking about, well, everything, but mostly I am thinking about Stan. I am thinking about the night that Stan was here in my house, in my bedroom and in my bathroom. He was naked in my shower. He looked so beautiful and so alluring, like a poisonous apple.

I still wish that I gave into him. I would have felt pleasure for a while at least. I probably would have woken up alone and hurt, but at least I would have had a man to love me for a little while, but now I had none. It is depressing. I cannot go back; I tell myself this.

Oh, hocus-pocus, Mary Beth. Get up and get dressed. Go to work.

I get up and I make my bed. I take a hot shower. I put on makeup and cover up my face and my cut-up lips. I get dressed. I walk downstairs and make breakfast for myself and then I dash out the door.

Oh Boy! When I arrived at work, I was not prepared to see what was going on. It was unbelievable!

I got to work and parked my car like usual. I was walking into the building and then up the stairs to my office, and then I saw it. Some lady was in Stan's office. I have never seen her before.

What is the purpose of her being here? Is she new? Who is she? A new intern perhaps? She is young and beautiful. Legs for days. What kind of legs do I have? I shave. I work out, well sometimes.

Everything about this woman is perfect—her hair, her clothes, her nails, everything down to her toes. I could see why Stan would give her attention, but he is married. Well, that has never stopped a man from cheating or Stan cheating on his wife with me.

I do not understand it. Who is she? I want to know. I have to know who she is. I have to find out. Is she replacing me? A new assistant, perhaps, for Stan.

I cannot believe my eyes. Doug appears from out of nowhere. I am stunned. Where had he come from? Had he been in Stan's office this whole time? What is going on in Stan's office?

I want to walk over there and find out, but as I start to walk out of my office and into the hallway, I stop in my tracks. I can clearly see that there are other women in Stan's office—several, in fact.

Oh, my gosh. Stan has turned our business into a whorehouse. I just know it. Is this the merger that they have been talking about? Oh dear. Is this legal? An escort service, really?

I get closer so I can hear and see more. I can hear Stan talking to one of the women.

"Mary Beth. She works for me. She is a nice person. I want you to meet her. You will be working with her. She is good at her job, and she is also, a good friend of mine, well"—he caught himself and cleared his throat— "work colleague."

What? I turn around and walk away. I do not want to hear anymore. I have to work with working girls.

Oh, my gosh. The bathrooms here will be X-rated when they all start working here. I will have to wipe down every surface that I touch. They are going to call me Mary Maid when I am done cleaning every inch of the women's bathroom and the firm for that matter.

I am utterly appalled. I walk back to my office and sit down in my chair. Next thing that I know, Stan and his new girlfriend stroll past my office. He is giving her the tour. I bet he is—the tour with a scenic route. Do not worry sweetheart the tour you are going on is a tour that will go on and on and on. He will give her the whole tour and leave nothing out. He has done that with me. Stupid me.

Oh well. That part is over. Or is it? I still do not want it to be. I will miss his touch and the attention he gives to me. I guess that is what would last. Everything else will fade away into the darkness. I would miss all of it when I went—if I do go.

What? Mary Beth, you have to leave this place. I have to leave Stan behind. Why do I crave Stan and his touch so badly?

I am curious as to why I have not heard back from the company I interviewed with last month. I am quite anxious to hear back from them. I hope it will be positive news. I have had too much melancholy to last me a lifetime. The pain is so real right now. Nothing makes sense to me anymore.

What am I talking about? Mary Beth, get a grip. Here they come. Shut up, Mary Beth. Breathe. Smile. Be confident.

"Hi, Mary Beth. Good morning. How are you doing? I would like to introduce you to one of your new work colleagues. She will be starting here very shortly. Her name is Abigail Greenvale."

"Hi, Stan. Good morning. I am doing well. Thank you for asking. Nice to meet you, Abigail.

"Nice to meet you, Mary Beth. I look forward to working with you. Stan has said that you do a lot of great work here." Abagail shook my hand. Her limp handshake did not impress me at all.

"Thank you very much, Abagail. I am sure that Stan did. Stan is a real charmer. I look forward to working with you as well. I am sure that you will be happy here. You will fit right in here. Won't she, Stan?" I am trying so hard not to sound sarcastic or let Stan know that I am mad at him or if I seemed a bit jealous of Abagail, but regardless I say this with a smile.

She will be working with me. What? Why do I have to work with her? What will I have to do? Train her? Throw some food at her or something. I mean she is so skinny. I have no idea what is going on here. Abagail Greenvale more like Abagail toothpick to me.

"Well, Mary Beth, we should be going. I still must show Abigail around the rest of the building. I will see you later. Bye." Stan was smiling at Abagail the whole time that Abagail and I were talking to each other. Gee, who could blame him. She was only half his age.

Stan and Abigail looked like the best of friends as they headed out of my office and down the hall. Yuck. Double yuck. Triple yuck. I want to puke.

After everything I have been through and what Stan has put me through, he thinks I am going to train that little whore? You have got to be kidding me.

Oh, why is my phone not ringing? Ring darn you.

I sit back down in my chair at my desk. I start to pound my desk repeatedly. I start to cry just a little. I put my head in my hands. I think that I am imagining things, but my phone is ringing. I pick my head up from my hands.

Yes, finally. They are calling and offering me the job. Please be the job that I wish to take me away from this nightmare. Please say yes!

I pick up my phone. "Hello. Thank you for calling Greenland, Howler, and Harrison. This is Mary Beth. How may I assist you?"

"Hi, Mary Beth. This is Kim Meadows calling from Courtland, Woodhall, and Frankland. How are you doing today?"

I have been waiting for this telephone call since last month.

I burst into tears on the phone to Kim. I have been dying to hear from Kim. I need to hear those precious words from Kim. Please tell me that I got the job so I can leave this all behind me and Stan too.

I try to stop my sobbing, but my tears will not stop. The tears just keep coming. All of my emotions empty out of my body all at once.

"I am calling you, Mary Beth because I want to let you know that we enjoyed meeting with you, and we wanted to offer you the position at our company. We want to know when you will be able to start if you accept this offer. We will be giving you a few days to think it over. I am going to email you all of the information that you will need to know about our firm and the position. I will also send you the job description. What is your email address and what is your cell phone?"

"Thank you, Kim. Thank you for calling me," I said. "I do not have to think it over. There is nothing to think about. I do accept your offer. I would like very much to work for your firm. I can start in a few weeks. I will have to give my two weeks' notice to my employer very soon." I give Kim my email address and my cell phone number.

Kim and I exchange pleasantries. We say goodbye to each other. I hang up the phone.

Wow! I am in a daydream. The nightmare is finally coming to an end. I can see the light at the end of the tunnel. I am so happy that I cannot stop crying. Wait until Stan finds out. I highly doubt that he will miss me at all, especially with his new toothpick working here now. I will be a thing of the past, most certainly.

CHAPTER 20

I am sitting at my desk. I am in pain. I do not know what day it is. I feel that time has flown by so fast. I cannot believe that I am about to leave another part of my life behind me. I doubt that it will ever leave me. I will always be tied to it somehow.

Who would have thought that I would have stayed with Stan for such a long time? I know that things will pop up every now and then to remind me of my past when I leave here. I just know it. I will not be able to forget any of this or Stan for that matter.

How do I even begin to let go? There is no end in sight.

I should write my resignation letter. I have never done this before. I have no idea what to say in a resignation letter.

As much as I do not want to leave this place, there is nothing here for me to make me stay. Stan has moved on with some hookers and a toothpick, and I have my desk full of paperwork and no alcohol to numb my pain.

I will always look through my door into his office—into his world where I do not belong. I will always live with the pain if I stay. There is no other way out but out the door and onto a new adventure.

I have no idea what I am getting myself into. Should I take a chance? Should I end it all here now?

I have so many memories. Some good, some bad. Can I really just get up and leave? No. I could not. It is so painful. I am so confused. I am a mix of sadness and anger. I do have every right to feel this way.

I worked the day away. It is now 7:30pm. I still have work to do, but I debate whether I should stay or not.

I really do not care but I decide I should stay and get my work done. I could use the money. I know they will give it to me. They have every time I have worked late so far.

After I finish all of my work for the day, I get up and grab my coat and my belongings and leave for the day. I do not see Stan when I am leaving.

My co-workers were talking nonsense at lunchtime in the break room about some fancy dinner or something tonight with the new clientele.

Oh well. No kiss goodnight for me from Stan. Actually, I am happy. I do not know why but I really am.

I decide to not write my resignation letter today, but I will tomorrow. I will think about it. I think it is for the best if I do leave.

The next morning, I am sitting at my desk staring at my draft email for my resignation letter. I came into work this morning determined to write it and put the letter on multiple people's desks including Stan's and Doug's desks.

Lunchtime finally came, and I am so hungry. I will have to wait on writing my resignation letter I suppose.

I head out of the building. Someone is following me, but I do not know it. I am too wrapped up in my emotions, in my thoughts. Why would I think that someone is following me? I have been so paranoid lately.

I travel down the street to where a lot of restaurants are. I am very picky about which restaurant I want to give my business to. Every restaurant around here is busy. I spot one restaurant. It is an Italian restaurant. Not the one that Stan and I had gone to the other night.

I wait in line to order takeout. I am told that it will be about twenty minutes. I am so hungry. Where is my food? It feels more like an hour and I still have not received my food. I do not want to stand anymore at the counter. I want to sit down at a table.

There are tables and chairs by the window. I walk over and I sit down at one of the tables. I do not care if they say something to me. I stare out the window. I am watching people walk by and then I see someone watching me. He is looking right at me.

Who is this person watching me? What is going on?

I turn away from the window and I walk back to stand at the counter. I finally get my food a few minutes later. I pay the cashier and I head back to the office. I walk as fast as I can. I look over my shoulder every now and then.

I have so much work to get done. I know I will be working late tonight. I would rather be home watching *Modern Family*, but I have made a career here and have contributed a lot to this firm. I guess I still want to do my job in some respect.

I get to the front door of the law firm building and I pull the door open but at the same time I feel this tug on my purse and then around my waist. I feel like I am being pulled backwards away from the door. I let go of the door and then the feeling is gone.

I see one of the security guards start to run to the door. I swear I feel something on my arm and see a person's hand for a quick second. I hope that I am imaging things. I start to freak out.

The security guard Steven Rudlack opens the door and approaches me. I am standing a few feet away from the front door. "Mary Beth, are you okay? I saw someone approaching you fast. That is why I came over here, but then he ran. Did he touch you or grab you?"

He! Steven the security guard, knew it was a *he!* Oh, my gosh. I am frozen with fear. I lose it. Everything and I mean everything came at me all at once. I have a nervous and emotional breakdown right that second.

"You said he. Oh no." A second later I fall to the ground. The ambulance is called. I have to go the hospital again.

I wake up in a hospital bed. I turn my head and see Stan sitting in a chair by my bedside to my left. I sit up and I see Doug talking to one of the nurses right outside of my hospital room. He seems to be in deep conversation with the nurse. I even see Mr. Mark Greenland for a minute.

Wow. What is all the commotion about? Since when was I so important to the firm. Well, I do have five high paying clients with the firm, and I did win my last two courts cases that awarded the firm a lot of money. I totally forgot about that. I laid back down on the bed and turn my head away from Stan. I fall back to sleep.

I am dreaming. Last week, I had to go to court because no one else was available. I swear that it had been a trap. I was being setup by the firm. They wanted to see how good I really was. If I did not do well, I would be given a bad review by my peers and I would not get a promotion or a raise.

I had two extremely hard cases to finish up. My firm was pressuring me to be the finisher. I had to make it happen. It was incredibly stressful.

My first court case was about a young girl who was kidnapped by her dad and then with my help was awarded custody back to her mom who happened to be a senator for the state of New York and her dad went to jail. The other case involved a malpractice lawsuit which injured several young children. There was a big fight in the courtroom between me and the pharmaceutical company, but in the end, I acquired enough evidence to support the injuries caused by the drugs that were used in order to treat the rare illness that the children were suffering from. All by myself, I gathered together the evidence by working long, hard hours. I made a deal to the pharmaceutical company so that they would take it and they did. The children that were injured were being evaluated and treated at the local hospital and the pharmaceutical company would be footing the bill until each child was fully recovered. I made the firm about 70 million dollars last week all by myself. Not bad, I think.

I wake up from my flashback. I look over to my left. Stan is still sitting beside me. He just looked at me.

Stan spoke first. "What is going on, Mary Beth? Why are you here in the hospital again? Is there something you want to tell me? Is there something I need to know? You have to tell me and not just because we are friends but because we know each other. I am your employer; I am your boss, and this keeps happening to you. How? Explain yourself to me. Tell me something. Tell me anything. What happened today?" Stan is clearly frustrated with me. He runs his hands through his hair and sighs loudly. The look he is giving me, and his behavior is just the same that it always has been for as long as I have known him. I am so used to his expressions and behavior by now that there is nothing more to say about either one.

"I…I don't know." I said softly. I am afraid of Stan. I turn my head away from him. I cannot bear to look at him.

"Of course, you know, Mary Beth. Look at me when I am talking to you. This is not a choice. Tell me. And tell me now." His voice is demanding. I can feel his breath on my neck. He is leaning onto the hospital bed so close to me. I know that tone of voice. He is for real this time. He wants to know the truth. He reaches out and grabs my arm and squeezes it so hard that I wince in pain, but I do not say a word for a very long time. Finally, I get the courage to speak to Stan while still having my head turned away from him.

"You know Stan. I just want to leave. I am so torn about the life that I have built for all of these years with you. I cannot seem to part from them or you. It makes me very angry and very depressed at the same time. I want to stay here with you Stan, I really do, but I want very much to leave this place and you at the same time and start something new. Do you understand at all about why I am feeling this way?"

Stan did not answer me right away, so I decide to turn my head and face him. He looks so upset. I can tell that he is hurt by what I have just said to him. He tries to speak to me, but he remains silent.

He releases my arm. He sits back in the chair. He pushes back the chair from the side of the hospital bed. He put in his elbows to his knees and then put his head into his hands. A few minutes later in pure frustration he walks out on me. I cannot believe he left me again.

I am left all alone again. This time, the tears flowed out of my eyes all on their own and down my cheeks. I did not stop it from happening. I let myself cry this time. I cannot fight these feelings anymore.

I was released from the hospital at 10:00pm. The night made me feel cold and different. The look on Stan's face made the decision for me. Now I know what I have to do next.

CHAPTER 21

I come into work the next day. It is Tuesday. It is just another day at work, and I am doing all right—as well as anyone could be after being so traumatized these last few weeks. I feel like it has been a year instead of just a few weeks.

I am on a mission. I have to leave. I do not want to leave, but I feel that this is the right time.

My gut is telling me yes, but first I need to have some breakfast. My stomach is growling. I ran out of my house so fast that I did not get a chance to make myself some breakfast. I need coffee or something.

Something is bothering me, but I cannot figure it out. I do not think it is about me quitting this job and moving on to my next job. My mind quickly turns to Stan. Yes, he would miss me, and I would miss him. I would miss him as a friend— as much as a friend as he is to me. I am so depressed.

I get to the office. I walk into the building and up the stairs as usual. I walk into my office and turn on the lights. I take my coat off and hang it up on the coat hanger on my door. I put my purse in one of my office drawers. I walk to the break room and find lots of food to eat. Thank gosh. It is my lucky day today. Someone went shopping. I have never seen so much food in my life—well, at work I mean.

I smell something. It is a familiar smell. I walk around the break room to find it. I am searching. I know that I am getting closer.

Aha! I found it.

It is a cake. A cake? What for?

Well, what does it say? I have no idea. It is scribbled. It is a vanilla sheet cake with white icing and strawberries and flowers decorated all over it.

Should I cut myself a piece? I take the lid off of the cake. Oh wait… what is this? Something catches my eye. Oh, my gosh! My name! My name is what is scribbled on the cake! What in the world?

Oh, no! I hear voices just outside of the break room.

"Have you seen Mary Beth?" Aidan Darling said.

"She's here. I think I just saw her walk this way," Vanessa Toddy said.

"I hope she is not in the break room. It is a surprise for her," Tina Heathrow said.

I hear the clicking of shoes and the voices growing louder. Oh, now what am I going to do. I am starving. How was I supposed to know about this? This is definitely not my fault.

I freeze. Somehow my hair gets caught in the cake, but I am not paying any attention to what I am doing at the moment. I place the lid back onto the cake. I quickly duck down underneath one of the tables and chairs right behind me.

Tina walks into the break room and calls out my name. "Mary Beth, are you in here? If you are, you need to leave. This is not the time for snacking."

Tina will not leave. She just stands there, tapping her foot and looking around the break room like she wants to scold me if she could find me. The nerve. I am not a child. I am a hungry. One little bite will not kill anybody.

Finally, Tina leaves the breakroom. I get up from underneath one of the tables. I walk out of the break room, but not before I place plenty of the free food on a paper plate.

I finally get back to my desk with my plate full of food, but the clock tells me that I have been in the break room for almost an hour! Yikes!

Oh no! I need to hurry up! I need to get my report done right away because I have a meeting—an important meeting. How will I explain myself if I do not get the report done on time? I will be in so much hot water.

I can just picture it all now in my head. I will end up sitting in Doug's office listening to him yell at me at the top of his lungs, and then he will force me to work late with no overtime pay. That would definitely suck.

Working late with Doug would not be fun at all. He would pounce on me every minute until I got the report done if it is late. I could just hear him now. That is why I have to hurry and type as fast as I can to get it done before Doug yells at me and asks me if it is finished when it is time for the meeting.

Through my open office door, I can hear someone say that the meeting has been canceled until further notice. Not too long after that, I hear another person say that the meeting is back on and will be held in a few hours. They said the projector is broken.

This report that I put together for the firm can take me up to three and a half hours to prepare. Thank gosh I can type and eat at the same time.

I turn on my radio. Music can always calm me down. I type and eat. I finally find the icing, which has started to harden in my hair. I freak out.

I lean back over my chair to get my box of tissues, but I knock over the lamp on my desk and my telephone in the process and on top of that I fall out of my chair, creating a very loud thud on the floor. Well, it was more like a bang because everything happened at once. I am lucky my computer did not fall on top of my head.

Thank gosh, no one came in and asked me what I was doing. I will never be able to think of an excuse as to why I have icing in my hair. I reach up for my desk edge and I finally pull myself together—just in time because Darla Partington from acquisitions comes walking into my office without knocking.

Darla tells me that the meeting is at 3:00pm sharp and that I am to have the report finished prior to the meeting. "And do not be late to the meeting," she said. "Or it will be your ass, not mine."

Thank you for that, Darla. I really enjoyed hearing that from you.

I say nothing to Darla. I just nod my head and smile. I get myself back on track as to what I was doing before Darla interrupted me. I type faster and faster. It is almost 3:00pm. I am typing so fast I swear that I see smoke coming from the tips of my fingers.

Stan pokes his head into my office, but I am just too busy typing. I avoid eye contact altogether with him. What does he want now? He leans up against my door. Is he trying to catch me off guard or is he trying to make me notice him? I have no idea what he is up to. I have no time to play games with him or to talk to him. I have to focus on my report now until it is done and then maybe I will decide to talk to him but not before.

For some bizarre reason, he is being insistent on getting my attention. To me, the lost, forlorn look of disgust he had given me at the hospital last night had said it all. What does he want now? Doesn't he have a job to do? Like bang one of those bimbos named Abagail and to leave me alone. Doesn't he see that I am really busy right now? Idiot.

"Mary Beth," Stan said to me, "I have been thinking."

Oh no. This cannot be good. I keep right on typing. I am not paying attention to what he is saying or why he is here in my office bothering me.

Stan knows full well that I need to finish this report and that I will be in a great deal of trouble if I do not get this report finished.

Darn him! I cannot believe he will not stop talking to me. Be quiet Stan I am trying to concentrate here!

Doug passes by my office a few minutes later and he looks into my office and then he stops walking.

Doug approaches my office door. Doug says, "Hey, Stan! What are you doing in Mary Beth's office? Do you not know that she oversees typing up one of the most important reports for the meeting and for the company we are having in the next twelve minutes? Come on, man, leave her alone. You have work to get done yourself, like printing out your reports, right? Hurry up, man. I am not going to be waiting on you like the other times. This meeting is at 3:00pm sharp!"

Doug stares at Stan and then he points a finger at him. A few minutes later, Doug disappears down the hall shouting at everyone that he encounters along the way.

Man, that boy has a high-pitch voice. Doug's voice makes me jump quite a few times out of my chair. I am sure that people down at Rockefeller Center can hear him shouting and will call and make a lot of complaints about the noise level that he is making right now.

I type so fast when Doug was arguing with Stan that I finished the report. I am so happy that I am done with this report. I do however realize that I have several typos and now I have to fix them. I cannot believe that Doug stood up for me. That just never happens or has ever happened. Wow!

Stan is still lingering in my office doorway. He is now turned away from me and is staring out into the hallway. Then he turned back towards me and looked over at me typing away and then back out of the doorway and then looked back at me again. After looking between the door and me a few more times, he left without saying anything to me.

I glance up and see him sitting down at his desk looking for his reports. He then makes his way over to the hallway printer where he is trying really hard to organize his reports. I watch as Stan picks up the wrong-colored folders. Then Stan proceeds to place his reports into the folders not realizing that the folders are wrong. Stan_continues to place his reports into the wrong folders for the next few minutes until he realizes that he is doing everything wrong. Thank gosh he did not look at me right then because I was laughing at him.

He keeps picking up a folder and putting papers into the folders, but he keeps putting the reports into the wrong folders more than once.

I am still laughing to myself. Stan is not even ready. I am done typing up my report. Now all I have to do is save the pages to the main hard drive, print them out, and put them together with letterhead. Then I am done.

This usually takes me just a few minutes to put together, so now I am refreshed and relaxed.

Stan is still typing and printing out his reports.

I can see Stan getting frustrated. I look up from my computer just now and I see Stan walking towards my office.

No way. I am almost done. There is only five minutes left until the meeting starts and I am not going to help anyone now. Stan approaches me regardless.

Stan says to me, "Mary Beth can you help me with putting my reports together please?" "Yes. Just let me get my report done first."

Why did I just say that to Stan? Gosh darn it all!

Stan walks out of my office and returns to his office.

Stan is sitting in his chair behind his desk when I make my way over to his office a few minutes later.

"Mary Beth, I am having problems saving my data to the main hard drive, and then my printer is not working for some reason," Stan said to me.

I said, "I find that extremely hard to believe Stan. If I can save my data to the main hard drive and I can print from my computer, then there should be no reason for you not to be able to save your data or print out your reports. Stan, what are you doing? We have the most important meeting of the year in less than five minutes, and you are bothering me with this? Can you not ask someone else like your assistant? I mean, come on. I still have some work to finish before the meeting," I said to Stan. I am really frustrated with Stan at this point.

Stan says to me, "Mary Beth. You know I would not ask you to help me if I did not feel like it was important to me. You know me. When do I ask you for anything when it comes to business? How many times have I asked you for help? Maybe five times at the most. Please stop giving me a hard time." He sighs loudly and puts his hands up in the air in frustration.

I suddenly feel bad for him. Stupid me. "Okay, Stan. Fine. I will help you. I will be back here in a few minutes after I finish putting my report together."

Stan relaxes and sits back in his chair and puts his feet up on his desk. I am disgusted. I am appalled. I walk out of his office without looking back at him.

Stan has a smug look on his face while sitting at his desk while for waiting for me to return.

CHAPTER 22

I walk into Stan's office and around his desk to his computer. I stand next to him. He moves to the side so I can get closer to his computer screen. He is looking at his computer screen and not at me. He is so close to me. I have to touch him. I put my hand on his shoulder ever so lightly.

All of a sudden, he snatches my hand that is on his shoulder and grabs my wrist. He picks me up and sits me down into his lap, he wraps his arms around me and encloses me into his embrace so tightly that I can barely breathe. I am face to face with Stan. I look into Stan's eyes. His eyes are filled with hunger.

We are face-to-face. My heart is beating so fast. I am out of breath.

What is he going to do next? What is Stan thinking? Did he plan this all along? I am incredibly vulnerable right now. What if he advances on me? What then? Everything just disappears around me.

I forget about the meeting. I forget about everything. The two of us just stare into each other's eyes. Somehow, we are telling each other words that do not need to be spoken. It is sort of romantic.

The mood grows dim between us. I look away from Stan. Silence. Complete silence. Neither of us speaks to one another. All you can hear are people outside of Stan's office talking loudly to each other. No one is paying attention to us. They are terribly busy getting ready for the meeting.

Stan decides to speak first. "I knew you would come over to my office and help me. I did this on purpose. I just want to hold you in my arms because I can and look into your beautiful eyes. It feels so good to hold you, Mary Beth. I miss this. I miss you. You cannot go to Massachusetts. I will not let you go."

"Stan, as romantic as this all is, I hate to bring it to your attention, but we have a meeting to go to now. You are going to be late because you are not finished with your reports yet."

Stan reaches over my shoulder and picks up something from his desk. "Here they are Mary Beth. I finished them hours ago." Stan shows the reports to me.

I have nothing to say to him. I am in shock. I am so angry with him. I try to slap him, but he catches my wrist.

Stan smiles at me as he continues to speak to me. "Do you not get it Mary Beth? I can never let you go. You are mine." Stan moves me closer to him—so close that our noses are touching, and our lips are lightly pressed together.

Stan said, "I love everything about you, Mary Beth. You are all want I want in a woman. I like running my hands through your hair. I like to look at your face and I love your sexy body. I wish that I could have you here right now. Do you still desire me, Mary Beth?" His smile is now touching his eyes.

I seriously want to scream. I try to move but I cannot. He has me right where he wants me. He has his arms wrapped around me so tightly. I do not wish to feel his breath on my face or smell his cologne in my nostrils. I do not want to hear his voice in my ear or have him look at me anymore. I am totally disgusted with him, and there is nothing I can do about it.

A voice comes over the loudspeaker that makes us both jump up out of his chair. Doug shouts, "Everybody listen up, the meeting is about to start, and no one is here in the conference room and I am waiting. I want everyone to move their asses into the conference room now! Everyone better have his or her reports and presentations ready, or there will be a huge handout of pink slips before everyone leaves tonight. Do I make myself clear?"

Stan does not care. Stan shrugs his shoulders and waves his hand at the loudspeaker. He quickly turns his face back to me and gives me a look that could melt butter.

Oh help!

I try to get out of Stan's grasp but then he lowers himself back into his chair and places me back on to his lap again. He still will not let go of me. I stare at him and he stares right back. So, he wants to play a game? Ok. I will play—the only way I know how. His.

I start to relax and loosen up my body, and Stan feels that my body is starting to relax against him. I want him to think that I am giving up control, but I really am not.

He grins at me and then loosens his grip on me just a notch. I lean into him.

CHAPTER 23

Just as I am getting my way and sort of taking control of the situation, Doug shouts into the loudspeaker again, "Everyone, it is time for the meeting. Get your asses in here now if you do not want to lose your job!"

We are still lingering in each other's embrace. This feels so nice. I am having mixed emotions though. I am hot and aroused but I know that this is completely wrong. Staying here on Stan's lap will only lead to bad decisions. It will only fuel his ego more.

I move closer and closer into Stan's face regardless of the consequences. I feel the impact. The kiss is hot. The embrace is so steamy. Neither one of us let go.

We sit in our embrace and take it all in. I start to realize that I do not want to lose this job because maybe I still want to stay here and maybe he is the one who wants to lose his job. I maneuver my body on his lap so that he will loosen his grip on my waist. It works!

I squirm off Stan's lap and make a beeline towards the door. I run into my office, pick up my report and run to the conference room where everyone is waiting—or so I thought.

I make it to the door of the conference room and look in. Very few people are in the conference room.

Do I have the wrong conference room?

What is going on? Is this some kind of joke?

I said out loud to whoever is listening to me in the conference room, "Are you kidding me right now? I ran down the hall to not be late to this important meeting and now I am out of breath and Doug is not even here!" I am so pissed off right now. What a little bitch he is!

It turns out that Doug is late, and he is not ready for the meeting. Doug will not shout that over the loudspeaker now will he. Idiot. Maybe I should. Doug should be the one handed a pink slip and lose his job and not one of us.

All of this shouting and bickering broke out all over the office building. It is crazy right now. The people who are in the conference room start yelling at each other. I turn around and I can hear people down the hall yelling.

I finally decide to walk into the conference room and find a seat and sit down. It is getting too loud in the hallway.

About twenty minutes later, people start pushing each other out of the way in order to enter into the conference room. Some people fight each other for chairs except for Doug and Stan.

Thirty minutes later, we all are sitting and waiting in the conference room for Doug and Stan. I am looking at the projector screen. The screen is showing pictures of our firm—photos of us, our building, and our offices. There are also photos about what we do for a living and all of the many high-priced, important clients that we support. There are also pictures of our client parties and our holiday office parties.

Leaving the best for last—are the photos showing the merger that just happened. Yep, you guessed it—the nine bimbos with Doug and Stan and the rest of the senior partners. I swear they are all full of themselves—seeing themselves as rich, good-looking, all-powerful lawyers. They will piss in their pants if I ever decide to become a whistleblower.

I am not paying attention to my surroundings after watching the screen of pictures repeat itself five times. I start to fall asleep but before I can do that I turn to my right and who is sitting next to me? Stan. I wake right up. He starts to talk to me, but I turn away from him.

Doug finally makes his way into the conference room and shouts, "Everyone shut up." Doug looks in my direction, but I cannot tell if he is looking at me or Stan. He looks really angry.

Doug walks over to the projector and starts showing us slides about our sales, and who our new clients are, how we can do better with the clients that we have and who he wants to acquire as clients, etc.

I am trying to pay attention to what Doug is saying, but all I can hear is Stan whispering dirty thoughts into my ears. I swat my hand at him, and he backs off.

Thank gosh. I think I hit him in the nose or the eye. I turn to look at him. He is rubbing his mouth actually.

I am glad. I smile to myself. I cannot take it anymore. I want to move, but there are no more chairs left, and it would look bad if I moved in the middle of the meeting even if there were any empty chairs available.

I wonder when we will be having an intermission. I am so bored and disgusted at the same time.

In the middle of the meeting, after about an hour and a half, I hear this loud noise. I could not place exactly where the noise is coming from, but it is quite close to me. I look to my left. Nothing. I look to my right. Oh, my gosh! It is Stan!

Stan is fast asleep, and he is snoring. He only has to give one of the most important speeches and presentations of the year to all of us and update the entire firm on the mergers and things to come, but he is sleeping. I cannot believe it. I just stare at him.

Without any hesitation, because I am so disgusted with him, I kick him right in his left shin. That woke Stan up fast. Stan bends down and massages his shin. I tell him to wake up and stop snoring.

"What? Who kicked me? Leave me alone. I am sleeping. I am so bored," said Stan.

Unbelievable. Doug is going to be so mad.

Another hour passes. Whose turn, is it? Mine. I stand up from my chair. I am really nervous, but I should not be.

I start by introducing myself and my title. Everyone says hello and claps for me. I start filling them in on what my report is about. I have several papers to hand out. I made copies of my report before Doug came into the conference room. I talked about the most important parts, which I had highlighted for myself.

I goof up a bit after ten minutes into my presentation. Some people sneer and snort, while others laugh at me. Doug is not pleased with me. I have never seen Doug be happy with me, so at this point, he could seriously kiss my ass.

I look over to where Stan is sitting, and he is still sleeping. I want to see his smile and for him to give me his support, but I have to keep going. I am so disappointed in Stan.

I finally finish my presentation. I turned my presentation around in the end and I look around the room at everybody. Doug is smiling at me for once and is clapping for me, along with everyone else. Wow!

Go me! I feel so accomplished. I nailed it. I am so happy. I am so proud of myself. I am on cloud nine. I feel like I am a star in the making.

Stan, however, is still snoring but not quite as loudly as before. He had better wake up now because his presentation is coming up soon. Of course, me being the nice person that I am, I want to kick him in his other shin. I would not mind in the least.

I am so sick of helping Stan. You do things because you want to do them, and not because of the rewards that you will get in return.

When will Stan do something for me out of the goodness of his heart and not think about what he should get in return or demand something in return? Didn't his bimbos do that for him? Did they not give Stan enough satisfaction?

I am tired of his bad behavior and his lies. I am through. I am going to put in my letter of resignation tomorrow morning. No more doubts or thoughts about it.

As hard as I have worked in my career and did not receive or be offered a partnership, or the pay, or the respect that I deserve after all of this time of being a great lawyer is ridiculous. I am fed up.

You can forget it Stan because I am through with you. Just looking at Stan disgusts me. He will probably get a fifty percent raise just for showing up. He works so hard for this firm my ass. Someone else will have to present his materials so that he can get his beauty sleep.

Oh, blow it out your ass, Greenland, Howler, and Harrison! I am sick of working hard for you! Find someone else!

I almost leave the conference room right then, but I do not. I am however, the first person to hightail it out of there when the meeting is finished.

Poor baby Stan—he missed out on talking. I am sure his ego will be pissed off. He loves making speeches where he can say that he is the one who can take all of the credit and that he does magnificent work.

Stan falling asleep however, saved us all from the drinking we would have done in the conference room during and after his speech and presentation. So, that actually is a good thing.

If you think that Doug is boring, Stan is so much worse. He will put you to sleep and you would not wake up for two whole days. Yes, it is that traumatizing.

After I leave the conference room, I go back to my office and put my report down on my desk.

Suddenly, I hear so much noise. I walk out of my office and back down the hallway towards the conference room.

Oh wow! Who would have thought such a nasty fight would break out after the meeting! Thank gosh I left when I did.

Turns out Brad hit Stan in the head with what looked like a stale loaf of bread because he snored throughout the whole meeting and did not have to give his speech.

Tina threw her red high heeled shoes at Kevin for gossiping about her and Ben sleeping together. It was not Kevin who told everybody however, it was Ben. Ben and Kevin are really good friends and tell each other everything.

Zachary got really nasty and tried to break a vase over Doug's head with the water and the flowers still in the vase because he was promised to be a part of the presentation, but Doug lied to him. Vanessa got in the middle of the fight between Zachary and Doug and tried to break it up, but she got hit in the head with the vase instead. There was a lot of blood.

Aidan, Vanessa, and Tina started to argue about whose hair was in the cake for my surprise party. Tina took her coffee mug and threw at Vanessa. The coffee was cold, but her suit got ruined and Tina's coffee mug hit Vanessa in the face. Vanessa tried to slap Tina, but Aidan got in the way and got slapped. Tina yelled at Vanessa for slapping Aidan. Tina attacked Vanessa and then they both started fighting and pulling on each other's hair. Aidan tried to break them up but got punched in the mouth. He had to go to the breakroom to get some ice for his mouth and his cheek. Aidan's jaw was really red.

This whole outburst started because Doug would not listen to anyone. Half of my co-workers wanted to make changes to the firm and the other half of my co-workers tried to tell Doug that they have contributed much more to the firm than what he thought they did; but he neglected to see their accomplishments.

Oh, the drama. From where I am standing inside the conference room, I can see Mr. Mark Greenland_is clearly upset with everyone.

Mr. Mark Greenland stands up from the conference room table after witnessing all of the drama. He walks over to one of the cabinets in the conference room and pours himself what looks like to be a glass of scotch and throws his head back.

Mr. Mark Greenland must have poured himself a couple more glasses of scotch after I went to help Vanessa with the cut on her head because when I turn around, he had just started to walk away from the cabinet and then he fell down face first on the carpet. Oh dear.

It is a complete disaster here in the conference room. The police and the ambulances arrive because Rebecca had come upstairs to find out what all of the commotion was about.

The police came into the conference room and started to take people's statements. People were handcuffed and dragged away cursing and screaming at each other. There is blood on the conference room carpet from the cut on Vanessa's head. And to top it off, Bill somehow took one of the paintings off one of the walls and tried to throw it at Doug but ended up hitting our boss, Mr. Mark Greenland in the face as he was trying to get up from the floor. Too bad about Mr. Mark Greenland. That must have hurt.

Mr. Mark Greenland started cursing and then swung his fist at Bill to try and punch him but then he fell face first on the carpet again. I am going to go out on a limb here and say that Bill will no longer be working here ever again.

Thank gosh. I swear Bill was always stealing money and other things from the firm, but I could not prove it.

I am upset about the painting though. I really liked that painting. The painting was a special gift from one of our regular nice clients. I wonder if I can find a buyer to buy a new painting. That will be my errand for tonight. The special part about the painting is that it was signed by the painter. So, I might add, it is worth quite a bit of money.

I stay in the conference room and clean up what I can after everyone has left the conference room.

I notice that Stan is no longer in the conference room when I am leaving. He is not in the hallway or in his office. He is nowhere to be found.

I ask Rebecca after I make my way downstairs to her desk. She said that the police questioned Stan but did not take him down to the police station. Rebecca told me everyone has been brought down to the police station except for me, herself, and Stan. Rebecca said there were a few police officers still here looking around the building, though.

Where is Stan? Where did he go?

CHAPTER 24

I am so wrapped up in myself that I do not even pay attention to where I am going.

How could Stan get away from his responsibilities? I have to give my speech, but he does not!

I am almost to my office when I hear some commotion. I think it is coming from another office.

I can see as I approach my office, even though there are no lights on in my office, except for the lights in the hallway, that someone is in my office, at my desk rummaging through my things.

Oh, my gosh! My purse! Someone is trying to steal from me. Not again. Thank gosh, if I scream this time, a police officer will come running. I know you are not supposed to scare a burglar, but I am so pissed off at this point to not to do *something*.

I turn around and walk into one of my co-worker's office, Anne Beers, remembering that she carries an umbrella to work every day, but forgets to take her umbrella home with her. I can use it as a weapon.

I walk into Anne's office, I pick up the umbrella, and then walk back to my office and peek inside.

The burglar is still in my office but now the burglar is sitting down at my computer. I walk as softly as I can into my office and over to my desk.

Aha! I injured the burglar. The burglar moaned like a baby. I hit the burglar again with the umbrella. The burglar grabbed my arm after I hit the burglar with the umbrella the third time. I start to scream so loud that I frighten myself. I get out of the burglar's grip and hit the burglar again with the umbrella.

I hear the police talking in the conference room down the hall, and I keep screaming at the top of my lungs until the police officers come to help me.

The police officers turn on the lights. I stop screaming and have to catch my breath. The police officers come into my office and walk over to where I am standing and start to ask me questions.

"What happened? What is going on in here?" said one of them.

"It looks like a burglary gone bad to me," said the other officer.

I start to speak, but all that I can think about is that I want an alcoholic beverage so bad right now.

"I was coming back from the conference room and I saw this person in my office. I could see that this person was rummaging through my desk and my purse. I caught this burglar on my computer as well. This burglar is wearing a mask and gloves." I point to the limp body sprawled across the floor behind my desk with his or her foot on my chair. I can see some blood seeping into my carpet.

"Are you hurt? Did this person attack you? Do you need medical attention?" said the first officer.

I look at him for a moment. I just stare at him and try to control my breathing.

"I am sorry, ma'am," he continues. "My name is Detective Kurt O'Donnell."

"Hello. My name is Mary Beth." The other officer introduces himself.

"Hi, Mary Beth. My name is Detective Samuel Cook. I am sorry that you have to go through this. Are you sure that you are, okay?"

"Yes, I am fine. Thank you for coming to my office so quickly. It was very scary. I need to sit down and drink some water." I take a seat in one of my chairs after I grab my purse from the burglar.

"Are you going to arrest this person?" I am searching through my purse to see if anything was taken. I point again, adding, "Could you search the burglar just in case he or she took something of mine? I would appreciate it. Thank you."

"Yes. Let's just see who it is first. Let's see if you know this person," said Detective Kurt. Detectives Kurt and Samuel went towards my desk to get to the unconscious body lying on the floor back behind my desk.

Do I really want to know who it is behind the mask? Can I face this person?

The two detectives stand on either side of the body and start to pat the burglar down. They find my driver's license, my wallet, money, papers of some sort, pictures, a small camera, and two cell phones.

One of the phones starts to ring. Then the ringing stops. Then there is a beep. It is a text message. The text message reads, "Is the job done yet? You know how. Remember what I told you. Keep it clean. Leave no trace. This is important."

Detectives Kurt and Samuel text back, "The job is done."

Then Samuel got paged over his radio, and then he left my office.

What was that noise? I thought I heard a loud noise. With all the commotion that has happened tonight, I cannot decipher anything right now. My head is spinning. I feel sick.

The cell phone beeped again. There is another text message from the phone. The text read, "I know the job is not done cop. Something will happen to you next. I warn you that it will end in blood for you."

Detective Kurt stopped cold. He froze.

I put all of my stolen belongings back into my purse. I grab my coat and start to put it on. Then I crouch down behind my desk next to the burglar who is out cold.

Detective Kurt called to Detective Samuel over his radio. No response. He tried again. No answer.

All a sudden, it is dead quiet. I hear footsteps. I whisper to Detective Kurt, "Someone is coming down the hall. What do we do?"

I am sweating so badly. I can hear the footsteps getting closer and closer to my office. My breathing is unsteady. My heart is beating so fast. I close my eyes and take a deep breath.

I open my eyes slowly. Detective Kurt is standing near the doorway and slowly closes the door and then turns off the lights and then motions for me to be quiet.

My desk was upgraded last week. It is a huge wrap around desk. It is a gift from Stan and Doug. A mockery gift though. More room on a desk guarantees more paperwork. Gee, how thoughtful.

Oh, no. The person is now inside my office. Oh, crap. I have to sneeze.

I smell something—a familiar scent. No, it could not be. It has to be an imposter.

It cannot be the one and the same, could it be? Is this the person responsible for everything that has happened to me so far?

No. I do not want to believe it. Whoever this person is probably wore the same exact scent. What are the chances?

The person starts to whisper. "They should have been outside by now. I have my men outside looking for them." I am scared.

The person closes the door to my office. Little light came into my office from the hallway. I do not know where Detective Kurt is.

The person on the floor starts to move. I hope I will not be found.

I see Detective Kurt then. He is trying to hide behind my filing cabinet in the corner of my office. He motions to me with his fingers, giving me an okay sign.

No, I am not ok. I am far from it. We are both going to die in my office. I just know it. I put my head down and close my eyes and try to squeeze myself more tightly into the corner of my desk.

Oh no. What happened? I hear a noise. The person comes close to where I am hiding but does not see me. The person has their back to me and crouches down in front of me. The person just lingers over the body on the floor for a while. Then the person stands up and kicks the burglar's body a couple of times and then punches the burglar in the face. I hear the burglar moan.

The person said something like, "Worthless piece of trash. What good are you?" The person is so quiet I can barely hear his voice.

There is no way for me to recognize the voice.

I can hear and see the person walk to the front of my desk and sit down in one of the chairs. I see some light like a cell phone. The person must be texting. I hear a noise and then the person stands up and leaves my office. I do not see who it is. I want to know who this person is so badly.

CHAPTER 25

As soon as the person leaves my office, I crawl out from underneath my hiding place. Officer Kurt helps me up from the floor. He asks me if I recognized the person or recognized the voice. I tell him no.

Officer Kurt turns the lights back on and then calls for backup. Other police officers walk into my office and handcuff the burglar and take the burglar away. The other police officers said that they found Detective Samuel knocked unconscious in another office down the hall. They took Detective Samuel to the hospital.

I walk down the hall to the ladies room to get paper towels, water, and soap to try and clean up the blood on my rug.

I definitely will be planning on giving my notice tomorrow. I will not hesitate to write my resignation letter as soon as I walk thorough my office door tomorrow morning.

Tomorrow I am going to leave work early and I am going to put my house on the market. My house should sell fast. The house is nice and big. I will be living in Massachusetts in a few days. I cannot wait. I will call Kim and tell her that I will be coming sooner than planned and that I can start right away.

The police insist that I go to the hospital just to make sure that I am ok.

I am waiting in my hospital room when the doctor comes in.

"Hi, Mary Beth. My name is Dr. Anthony Prince. I will be taking care of you this evening. It turns out that I have reviewed your charts and tests, and you seem to be fine. You might still feel weak, so I will be monitoring you here overnight while we run more tests. Do you have any questions?"

I shout at Dr. Prince. "Why am I here? What is going on?"

Dr. Prince's voice is calm. "Because of the trauma that has happened to you over these past few weeks including the car accident where you hit your head, it is best that we make sure that you are in good health. I just want you to rest now. You are going to be alone in this room. No one will disturb you. There are police officers sitting outside your room to protect you tonight. Please do not be scared. You are safe here. I have to look over my other patients right now, but I will return to check on you later on tonight."

"But this doesn't make any sense to me. I feel fine. I might be exhausted or dehydrated but I want to go home and sleep in my own bed," I scream at Dr. Anthony Prince.

"I understand your concerns, Mary Beth. It is best that you stay here at the hospital and rest now. Please order something to eat and drink like you would normally at home. Just push the button, and the nurse will be with you shortly. If you want to watch TV, feel free to do so." Dr. Anthony Prince glanced down at his watch. Mary Beth, I will see you later on tonight. Please be sure that you try and relax." And with that, he smiled and waved goodbye to me and turned on his heels and walked out the door, making sure the door closed all the way.

I am hungry and a bit thirsty. I will order food and something to drink. Too bad that I cannot have any alcohol.

I turn on the TV and flip through the channels. Oh, thank gosh. I find my favorite TV show. Yeah! I smile a little and breathe a sigh of relief. *Modern Family* is on. I can relax now. And what is best is that it is an all-day marathon. Now if there weren't any commercials, that would be much better. I laugh really hard.

I am still laughing when my nurse named Sandy comes in and brings me my food and my beverage of choice. She sets up the tray for me. She goes about her business, taking my vitals and standing before me and performing other nursing tasks.

"It is so good to hear you laugh and to see you smile, Mary Beth. Keep it up. We will be doing some more tests tonight, maybe in about another hour or so."

"That's fine. I am having a good time watching Modern Family."

Sandy smiles and turns around and walks out of my hospital room. I smile and laugh for another two hours. Then it is time for me to do more blood tests and another segment of X-rays and other tests.

I get back to my hospital room about 9:00pm. The clock on the wall tells me so. The marathon is still on. I laugh and smile until the marathon ends. I turn off the TV. It should be a better day tomorrow. I still need answers to my questions. Maybe tomorrow I will get them. I fall asleep. I start to dream of the handsome Dr. Anthony Prince. I smile while I am sleeping.

CHAPTER 26

I wake up in the middle of the night. I do not know what time it is. I feel like there is someone in my hospital room, but it is not a doctor or a nurse. I get this creepy feeling inside of me. Am I going to be murdered here in the hospital? I am just about to transform my life into something better. I do not want to die. I am not ready. I am too young.

I can see a shadow move in the corner of my hospital room. Is the shadow moving closer to me or away from me?

The shadow is actually moving closer to me. Oh no. What do I do? Where is the nurse button? What button do I press to make some noise so that this person will go away and leave me alone and not murder me?

I am able find the nurse call button and it beeped. Thank gosh.

I hear a noise and then the door to my hospital room closes. Oh my gosh! I am not dreaming or seeing things. The nurse on duty comes into the check on me a few minutes later. She gives me some sleeping pills and then I fall back to sleep.

The next morning Nurse Sandy and Dr. Anthony Prince are talking near my bed. They are reviewing my tests. They exchange looks. It does not look good. What is wrong with me now? They said that I was fine last night. What broken bones? I feel fine. I feel even better because I have food and water in my stomach. Oh, no. Maybe I should pretend that I am asleep. Then, nurse Sandy leaves the room.

I want to go back to sleep and dream. I want to dream of sugarplums in my hair and dancing in the air. I want to be some place where I can be happy. Is there such a place? I wonder.

Dr. Anthony Prince walks over to my bed. I try to hope for the best and prepare for the worst. Dr. Anthony Prince said, "Mary Beth it appears that you are fine. There are some minor contusions and abrasions to your body but there is nothing that will not heal properly. Your blood tests came back healthy. Nothing out of the ordinary. Nothing to be concerned about. However, I am going to prescribe some sleeping pills for you since you are having a hard time sleeping from all of this trauma that you have endured. I am going to call it into the local pharmacy, and you can pick up your medication once you leave here. The police want to make sure that you are alright so they will be escorting to the pharmacy and then back to your house. You should be able to leave here in a few minutes. How are you feeling Mary Beth?"

I said, "I am fine. Thank you so much for all of your help, Dr. Anthony Prince. Goodbye."

CHAPTER 27

I finally get released from the hospital. It is about 1:00pm. I hate hospitals. I hope that I do not have to go back to any hospital for a long time.

I am assigned to two nice police officers who escort me to their police vehicle. They drive me back to my job so that I can pick up my car. I am driving my car to the pharmacy to pick up my medication and the police officers are following closely behind me.

The police officers escort me back to my house. I pull into my driveway and put my purse on my shoulder. I have my coat on. I am sort of hot.

I tell the police officers that I am expecting someone to come and look at my house later on today. I tell the police officers that I am putting my house on the market and moving back to Massachusetts.

I managed to make the phone call to the local realtor when I was at the hospital early this morning.

I tell both of the police officers that I have landed a new job. I tell the police officers that I am happy. I tell them that I want to leave all of this horrible stuff behind me for good.

Both police officers want to do a perimeter check outside house first and then take a walk around inside my house. They want to make sure that I am safe.

I feel safe. I feel happier now that I know that I am moving on and getting away from Stan.

I lock my car. I walk to my front door and unlock it. I put my keys, my purse and my coat down on my kitchen table.

I want to eat real food. I want to have a glass of wine. I still can because I have not taken my medication yet.

I walk over to my refrigerator and take food out and place the food on my kitchen counter. I am starting to make myself a sandwich when both police officers come into my house from my backyard.

Detective Ethan Murphy said, "Everything looks safe. Nothing seems suspicious. Now we will go take a look around the inside of your house. Will that be, ok?"

I said, "Yes. Of course. Thank you."

Detective Steve White said, "You have a nice garden out in your backyard. Do you know what flowers are planted in your backyard?"

I have no idea to what to say. "I think they are marigolds. They were already planted in my backyard when I bought this house."

Both Detectives Steve and Ethan turn around and walk away from me to go and inspect my house.

I walk back into my kitchen to finish making myself a sandwich. My back is to the front door and to my living room. I am spreading the mustard on my second slice of bread with a knife when I feel a hand cover my mouth and a voice telling me to not make a sound and to drop the knife and do not attempt to scream.

I freeze. I drop the knife onto the counter. The person's voice is muffled. The person is wearing gloves. The person puts a blindfold over my eyes, and then the person ties my hands together in front of me with cable ties.

The person picks me up and carries me outside of my house and places me into the trunk of a car. I hear the trunk close. The car starts to pull away from the curb.

I can hear the police yell stop as they are trying to run after the car. I can feel the car speeding away. I can hear the tires screech. I am so afraid.

What is going to happen to me now?

Will I survive?

CHAPTER 28

The car stops after what seemed to be an exceedingly long time. I hear the trunk open. The voice says, "There you are beautiful. Now I have you all to myself."

Oh no. I pass out.

I wake up to find myself lying on my left side on a sofa that is red with a flower pattern on it. I am facing the inside of the couch. I can see that the couch is old. There are holes in the sides of it. My hands have been untied and my blindfold has been removed.

I can see it is a house. I am in somebody's house! Who's house? Oh, my gosh! I do not recognize anything. Where am I?

I hear chopping noises behind me. The voice says, "Are you hungry? Do you want something to eat?"

Is he talking to me? How did he even know that I am awake? I hear footsteps behind me, but I do not want to turn and face my kidnapper.

"Hello Mary Beth."

Oh my gosh. I cannot believe it. I know that voice.

It is Stan! Stan kidnapped me! Oh my gosh!

I feel so powerless now. I am paralyzed with fear. I cannot move. I cannot breathe. Can Stan really be the monster that I never thought that he could truly be? I start to cry.

"*Cat* got your tongue Mary Beth. I understand. You were always a thinker. Have you figured it out yet? I always thought that you were smart. The police will not find us. Well, they will not find you actually. I thought that I was clear when I said that you were mine. That I loved you and that I want to take care of you. No one else is going to have you Mary Beth except me. Not those police officers or that doctor from the hospital. Not Anthony Whitmore. Not even Doug."

"Doug?" I whisper to myself. What is he talking about? I thought Doug hated my guts. Stan is insane.

Stan said, "I want you to eat something Mary Beth. I need you to be strong and not keep passing out on me. Do not worry about clothes or anything else. I have brought everything that we will need until I am through with you. It could be a few days, or it could be a few years. Depends on my mood and how you behave towards me. If you run, I will catch you. You're not going anywhere Mary Beth until I say so."

I said, "Stan? What happened to you? Why are you being so cold to me? Why am I here?"

Stan said, "If you have been listening to me the whole time that I have been speaking to you Mary Beth than you would not be asking me any questions. I want you Mary Beth and only you." Stan's voice grew harsher by the minute as he spoke to me.

I said, "I don't understand. What about your wife and your kids? What about my job? What about my new job? People will want to know what happened to me."

Stan said smugly, "I told our firm that you are leaving and moving back to Massachusetts for a new job. So, they told me goodbye for you. I also told the firm and my wife and my kids that I need to have a vacation by myself for a while. And of course, how can I forget, the new firm that you got a job with located in Massachusetts. I called them and told them that you changed your mind. Yes, they were really heartbroken especially Kim your dear *friend*. You have no job anymore Mary Beth, so you are stuck with me. You have to depend upon me now."

Stan almost shouted at me. "Mary Beth, in case you have not realized it yet, I can have my way with you any way I want to. And there is nothing that you can do about it or to make me stop now."

I am in shock. I said, "It was you this whole time? Why? I want no part of this Stan!" I sit up on the sofa and then I try to run away but Stan grabs me and pushes me hard back down on the sofa. He grips my face in his both of his hands and forces me to look at him eye to eye.

Stan said, "Look at me Mary Beth. Yes, Mary Beth. All of this was me. I did it! I hired people to make you miserable. To frighten you. To make you paranoid. And to hurt you of course. Sometimes it was me and sometimes it was the people that I hired. Do not think for a second that you will ever be able to prove anything against me Mary Beth. No. I cannot let you do that to me Mary Beth. I believe that you are going to beg me to ease your pain. You will wear yourself down to the point that you will beg me to help you either with pleasure or pain but let us eat some food first. Do not fight me or you will lose. No slapping me this time Mary Beth."

Stan grabs my arm and pulls me off of the sofa. He drags me to a table with chairs. He places a plate of food in front of me. He also places a glass with liquid next to my plate. I think it is milk. He gives me a fork but no knife. I do not know if I would have used it or not even if he had given me a knife. I have to eat what he puts in front of me. It is not bad, but I have no taste in my mouth. I have no appetite at all. I am being held against my will. There is no one to help me now. I am trapped. I try not to cry but it is no use. What will that do?

Stan is sitting next to me at the table and hands me some napkins. He says, "Remember Mary Beth when you break apart, I will be the one giving you tears of pure pleasure and satisfaction and not sorrow. And maybe pain here and there." Stan winks at me.

Stan always has a way with words. Idiot.

When we are both done eating, he takes our dishes and places them into the kitchen sink. He grabs my arm again and drags and pushes me up a flight of stairs. He pushes me into one of the bedrooms. We walk through the bedroom into the bathroom. He takes a washcloth from the rack on the wall and turns on the water. The washcloth feels nice and warm as he presses it against my mouth. He makes me wash my hands with soap and water. He dries my hands with a towel.

Stan leads me out of the bathroom and onto the bed. He pushes me down gently onto the bed. He takes off my shoes. He pushes me back so I that I am laying down on the bed. He tells me to stay still. He walks to the other side of the bed and ducks down underneath. What is he looking for? What is he doing?

He walks back to the side of the bed where I am lying down. He gets on top of me.

I close my eyes. I cannot believe that this is happening to me. I want to make myself think that this is all a dream.

"Wait a hot minute, Stan. I am not broken yet. I am not ready. I am telling you no Stan. Get off me Stan!"

Stan said, "Fine. Have it your way Mary Beth. It will only be a matter of time though. I will win in the end. *Just you wait and see.* Just remember it was you who lied to me."

Stan rolls off of me onto the other side of the bed.

What on earth is Stan talking about? Oh my gosh. The paper with the secrets. Is that what he is talking about? Is this the reason why I am here?

I just lay on the bed on my back staring up at the ceiling. I feel so numb. I fall asleep eventually, but I am so scared to. I wake up every now and then to make sure I still have my clothes on, and he is not on top of me. I thought maybe Stan would do something to me while I slept and thankfully, he did not.

Stan is actually taking care of me and feeding me. I am Stan's prisoner. He lets me bathe alone. He did give me a toothbrush, toothpaste, floss and Listerine. He is waiting to strike. He is waiting for the right moment. He does not try and touch me. Thank gosh!

There is a couch in front of the TV downstairs. He lets me watch TV sometimes, but he always sits next to me on the couch and puts his arms around me.

After eight months, I start to fight with Stan physically. He wants to bed me so badly. I scratch him and slap him. He grabs my hands and puts them behind my back. I lose every time. The only time that I won was when I threw a beer in his face at dinner one night. He gave up fighting with me, but he was so mad at me.

Stan accuses me of stealing the piece of paper that had flown into my office that one night and that I was going to use it against him. I said yes, I took the stupid piece of paper and that I was going to tell on him right before I left for my new job in Massachusetts. That was how the fight started. All of the other fights were just set off by boredom or by rage. I am so unhappy that I am his prisoner, and he is so unhappy that I do not desire him.

Twelve months have gone by. I just cannot hold out any longer. I just cannot fight it anymore. I guess I have to give into Stan. I have to give into his wishes. I do not want to, but I just do not have any more willpower left in me.

Stan must be put something into my drink or my food to desire him every day. I never get to handle the food or pour myself a drink.

I remember how it started. Stan got drunk at dinner time and then he got violent. He started yelling at me and then he punched me right in my face. He picked me up from the table and carried me upstairs to the bedroom. He put me down on the bed and got on top of me.

He said that he was sorry that he had punched me in the face downstairs in the kitchen. He said that would not happen again. He said that physically assaulting me was the last thing that he wanted to do to me. He tried to calm me down. He was apologizing over and over to me. He kissed my tears away. He was saying sweet things to me.

Then Stan started to whisper into my ear suddenly, "You want me. I know you want me Mary Beth." Stan said this to me over and over again until I went completely limp in his arms. His voice was possessive and full of hunger.

I give up. Stan has won again. I am totally broken. My world is crumbling down around me. I cannot fight Stan anymore. Stan's needs are now my needs. He starts to kiss me, and I lose.

I regret every minute of it, but somehow my body felt pleasure in the midst of all of it. At some point during the night, I did start to feel pain. It felt like a burning pain. My face hurts so much. I cry so many tears during the night.

The night did not end. Over and over again, Stan would wake me up until his satisfaction was complete. Stan fell asleep next to me on his stomach with his hand across my stomach, gripping me so hard like a weapon, like I was his possession now until forever.

I saw a knife on the other side of Stan as he slept. Would he cut my throat?

I cannot believe this. I am so upset with myself. It has been a year now. One year has gone by and the police still have not found me yet. I wonder if they ever will.

I want to go home. I want to get away from Stan. That night that we were together still haunts me. I try to not think about it. My face still hurts. Stan gave me an ice pack, but my face is still swollen. My lips have stopped bleeding though. Stan put a band aid on my bottom lip.

Regardless of what happened between us, Stan reminds me of it every day. Stan did pour all of the alcohol down the drain the next day though. He told me that he would. At least he did not lie to me about that.

The sex between me and Stan was consensual. It was not rape or sexual assault. I did desire Stan. I said yes to Stan. I do not want it to happen ever again even though, my body is betraying me at every minute of every day that I am stuck here in this house with Stan.

I cannot take it anymore. If I stay here any longer it will happen again. No. I cannot let it happen again. I try to escape the very next night.

I feel a very strong grip on my shoulders as I am trying to unlock the front door. I turn around. Stan is really angry at me and points a knife at me. He puts the knife to my chin. I can feel pain. I feel that I am bleeding. Stan is breathing heavy. He finally calms down after a few minutes.

"What am I going to do with you Mary Beth? Oh, I can think of one thing that would satisfy us both. Do you know what I am thinking about? You enjoyed it the last time. I am sure that you will again. Come here. Do not fight me." He gives me a wicked grin.

Stan places the knife into the kitchen sink. He says that he will not be needing this anymore. He snickers at me. He has one hand gripping my shoulder like a vice as he places the knife in the sink. I hear a clattering sound as he drops the knife into the sink. I jump. I am really scared now. Will he really kill me? I shudder to think. My mind is racing.

Stan suddenly pulls me into his arms, and he picks me up and puts me over his shoulder before I can slap him. He carries me up the stairs and brings me back into the bedroom and places me down on the bed. He gets on top of me and starts kissing my lips. He starts to touch me and massage me all over through my clothes.

He gets off of me. He stands up from the bed and grabs my left leg and takes off my sock and then he grabs my right leg and takes off my other sock. I still do not know what Stan did with my shoes.

He runs his nail on the underside of my foot. He does the same thing with my other foot. I feel something to start to take control of me. How does he do this to me? I feel my body start to slowly betray me.

How do I fight him off? How do I end this torture? I do not want to do this again. Help!

He gets on top of me again and straddles me this time. He starts to unbutton my blouse. He says to me, "I want you, Mary Beth. I want you to look at me Mary Beth. I want you to watch what I am going to do to you. I want to see your facial expressions when I go down your whole body."

His voice is so deep and sensual. I slowly open my eyes and look at him. He continues to unbutton my shirt. He spreads my blouse open. He bends down and kisses my lips, then he kisses my neck. He bites one of my ear lobes.

He puts his hands to my chest. I am starting to pant. I cannot control my body. He pulls up my t-shirt all the way to my neck that I have on underneath my blouse. He starts to kiss me below my bra and all the way down to my navel.

"I can feel your breathing change Mary Beth. I know that you want this too. Keep still."

He starts to unbutton and unzip my pants.

I am freaking out now. I try to kick him. He catches my legs and throws them both back onto the bed.

He pulls off my pants and drops them to the floor. He undresses himself. He is naked now except for his boxer shorts. I am still wearing my t-shirt and blouse and underwear.

He reaches down to his pants pocket and pulls out a condom. I am breathing really hard now. He gets back on top of me.

He whispers into my ear, "Are you ready for me?"

I panic. What do I say? I have to take back the control. I have to stop this. I have to calm down. I take a deep breath.

I look into Stan's eyes, I said, "I have to pee Stan."

"Are you serious Mary Beth? Really? Right now?" He is pissed.

"Yes. Stan I really have to pee."

"Fine Mary Beth. You can use the bathroom. Hurry up."

Stan gets off of me and helps me up from the bed so I can use the bathroom. I close the door behind me. I am about to lock the door.

Stan shouts to me, "Do not lock the bathroom door Mary Beth!"

"Well doesn't this suck apples and oranges!" I mutter to myself underneath my breath. I do not want Stan to hear me.

I am washing my hands when I hear noises. I quickly dry my hands on a towel hanging on the wall.

I open the bathroom door to find the police yelling at Stan. I jump. Thank gosh. It is about time.

Stan sees me after I have opened the bathroom door.

He gets out of the police officers grip as they are trying to handcuff him. Stan runs right at me and punches me right in the face…again. I am knocked backwards and hit my back on the sink. Something crashes to the floor. Something broke. I am in so much pain. My heart is broken. My heart broke. My heart is what made that loud crashing sound. I know it.

I slowly close my eyes and slump down further down onto the floor of the bathroom. I am laying down on the bathroom floor on my left side of my body crying my eyes out until I pass out.

Two police officers rush over to me a few minutes later after they have Stan in handcuffs and have led him out of the house.

The police officers gently wake me up and want to know if I am ok. I say yes. The police officers want to take me down to the police station to find out what happened to me but first the police officers want to take me to the hospital to get checked out.

The police officers make sure that I am stable and then they both let me get dressed by myself in the bedroom with the door closed. I dress myself as fast as I can. I find one sock, but then I cannot find my other sock. My head hurts. I can see my own blood dripping onto the carpet. I go into the bathroom and clean up my face and blow my nose. Ow! That really hurt!

I have to take a minute to before I can bend down to look underneath the bed and find out where my other sock is and then put it on. My shoes! Oh yeah! There they are. Stan put my shoes underneath the bed. I thought he threw them out in the garbage.

After I get dressed, I walk around the entire house searching for anything that might belong to me. I cannot find anything. I feel so sick to my stomach. I am in another bedroom and I see that there is a bathroom. I end up vomiting in the toilet for a while. I have to get out of this house. I really should go to the hospital.

I take my time walking out of the bathroom, the bedroom, the hallway and then I slowly take my time walking down the steps.

Finally, I walk outside to freedom. I can breathe the fresh air and I can feel the wind on my face. It feels good.

I can see that there are ambulances and police officers everywhere. I can see the police tape when I step outside of the house and down the front steps. The police roped off an entire block.

I walk over to a car on the street that is parked near the house. I lean up against the car. I take deep breathes. I feel dizzy. I feel light-headed. I place the tissues from my pocket to my chin, my face and my lips.

I see Dr. Prince to my left. What a nice doctor he is. He has come to check up on me.

He shouts to me that he wants me to make an appointment with him tomorrow morning at the hospital. I give him a weak smile. I am in so much misery. I am so traumatized at this point that I do not know up from down. Is this nightmare finally over with?

I look behind me and there is Doug. What is Doug doing here? He is shouting and waving to me from behind the police tape. He is smiling at me. I give Doug a weak smile as well. Maybe things will change and be better after all.

I turn back around, and I look straight ahead of me. My smile vanishes. I am looking at Stan. I see Stan is standing next to a police car. Stan is dressed in his clothes and his shoes. He is handcuffed. He is about to be placed inside the police car. I am so happy, but I do not show my happiness on my face.

The look on Stan's face is of pure hate. His eyes have razor blades in them again. Stan hates me, but I just stare right back at him with no emotion at all on my face. I hope that I do not ever have to see his face again, but I swear that I he mouthed some words to me.

This is not over. See you soon Mary Beth.

EPILOGUE

I feel so weak. My knees give out as soon as I see Stan being placed inside the police car. I am on my knees on the pavement. I breathe and then I close my eyes.

A couple of police officers approach me and help me up and walk me over to the ambulance. They want me to go to the hospital right away. I hear voices and then I hear sirens and then I fall asleep.

I wake up in the hospital and I am alive. I feel much better. I feel like so much weight has been lifted off of my shoulders. I can live my life again. The way I did before Stan got his hands on me and controlled my whole life. New beginnings. That sounds so nice. I smile to myself.

In the end, I found out that Stan had a serious gambling problem that got so out of control that he owed a lot of money to a lot of bad people in different states. These people ended up threatening his wife and his kids and that is the real reason why Stan did not leave his wife. He needs her money. He thought that his wife and her family would give him the money to pay back his debt. Nope. He thought wrong.

Stan's wife, Holly, ended up divorcing him after he was arrested after kidnapping me. I never knew her name until now. Holly was not told of the other things that happened inside the house. Holly ended up taking their kids back to Massachusetts to her parents' house where she got full custody of both children. She said in a statement to the police and to the news media that Stan's debt was his own problem, and he will have to find a way to pay back the money on his own. She also said that she has been through enough and so have their children. Holly wants nothing to do with Stan anymore.

I found out the firm Courtland, Woodhall, and Frankland was not a rival after all. It turns out that the firm did not hire Stan after he applied for a job there. He was so jealous and angry when he found out that I got offered a job there. I really am a better lawyer than Stan. I am so happy to have found out about that.

Stan kidnapped me to hide from his debt collectors, but also to have me as his possession. Two birds with one stone.

The house that Stan held me captive in was a house that his family rarely used in the summertime. It was in his wife's distant cousin's name. That is why it took the cops so long to find us.

I also came to find out that Stan had a love hate relationship with me. He really wanted to be with me, but he hated the thought of losing his power when he was with me. He had to have total control. He loved playing games with me. He wanted me to be weak with need. He wanted to break me.

He loved me one minute and then the next he did not. He did not want to feel that he needed me, so then he would change his behavior towards me and become nasty to me, but then he would change back because he loved me and that he missed me.

He just wanted me to be alone and needy. He wanted me to want him and only him. He turned everyone against me and isolated me. He wanted me to be in fear. He told lies to a lot of people about me, especially Doug. He wanted me to always come to him for protection and for help with everything. If he could not have me then no one else who could have me.

A few days later the police stopped by my house and told me that they had found enough evidence that would convict Stan of all of the crimes that he had committed against me. Wow! Unbelievable! This is such great news.

My house ended up not being sold after all. No one was interested in buying my house, so I decided to keep it regardless. I mean where else could I go?

I walked back into work after only two weeks later only to come to find out the truth about many other things about the firm.

Doug turned out to be a severe alcoholic and needed to go to AA. That was a bummer to find out, but it did explain a lot. I helped Doug through his problems, and he helped me through my problems. We became really close friends through our triumphs and tribulations together.

Mr. Mark Greenland and his son Harry had a serious cocaine problem. They both were arrested at the firm for possession and distribution of illegal substances.

The both of them were forcing their own clients and other employees at the firm to take the drugs and distribute them outside of the firm to make extra money. Every single one of them who made a sale had to give all of the money that they had made back to Mr. Mark Greenland and his son Harry to help out Stan with his gambling debts. Stan had found out about Mr. Mark Greenland's drug habits and Stan decided to blackmail them both.

Bill was indeed stealing from the firm; he also was arrested. He was taking money from his clients' accounts and using the money for his own personal uses.

That explains the yacht at the marina. It was the first party that I attended here at the firm. He was lying about how the yacht was an inheritance from his grandfather and that he was filthy rich. He was actually so poor. Turns out his grandfather was alive and only owned a rowboat and rented it out to the local fishermen at the dock right by his home during the summertime. All of the furniture on the yacht still had the price tags on them from Walmart no less and the yacht was not his. His friend let him use it for the night. Idiot.

They all ended up going to jail except for Doug. Doug had dropped out of the meeting about the firm who they were threatening to buy out if they did not keep quiet about Mr. Mark Greenland's and Harry's secrets. The firm is called Reed and Chess.

Turns out that Mr. Mark Greenland was planning on starting an escort service and a drug service through the firm Reed and Chess, whom he merged with in turn for their silence. The women that were in Stan's office from earlier on were secretaries from the firm Reed and Chess. Stan and Mr. Mark Greenland hired these women as executive assistants, which they were not qualified at all for. They barely knew how to use a copy machine let alone type. It was all just a cover up for what illegal criminal activities they were planning to do.

This is a lot to take in for one day. I drank a lot of wine that night by myself but not before I went to see Dr. Anthony Prince for my physical and I was given a clean bill of health. My face and lips have healed almost completely now. The rest of me probably will never heal.

It has been five months since I was kidnapped. I cannot believe it. I also cannot believe what happened last night. Doug came into my office and sat down in one of my chairs in front of my desk and told me that he wants to be there for me now and forever and to not ever leave my side. He told me he wants to me make me happy and I said yes. Was that a proposal?

Doug came around my desk and did propose to me. How romantic! I am so happy. I did cry but tears of joy this time. Doug hugged me and kissed me. It was so nice.

I sold my house soon after Doug proposed to me and I decided to move in with Doug because he asked me to.

A year later, Doug and I got married. Doug ended up taking over the firm of Greenland, Howler, and Harrison a few weeks after we got back from our honeymoon in Turks and Caicos.

Doug said I could continue working at the firm if I wanted to and understood completely if I chose not to. I said yes that I would like to stay on and work at the firm. Doug gave me a raise and a promotion a few weeks after I said yes, I would like to stay and work at the firm.

Doug later renamed the firm to Harrison and Strikker two weeks later. I was totally shocked. I am finally a partner! I am so happy.

Doug told me at work a few days later after he promoted me, that he knew Stan had been doing really bad work at the firm and that I was doing excellent work.

Stan somehow had stolen my work for his own. Doug told me that he found out that Stan had done the same thing to me at the Gold and Blackberry firm back in Massachusetts, but there was nothing that he could do at the time because Stan was doing the same thing to him and Stan was also stealing Doug's clients.

Doug confessed to me when we were working at the office late one night that he had liked me this entire time, for all of these years, and that he was sorry for his harsh words and his rude behavior towards me. He told me that he liked me when I came to interview at Gold and Blackberry, but Stan had stopped him. Stan lied to him in the conference room by the door. Stan told Doug that I had slept with my college professors during my college years to be able to graduate with honors and to get into a great law school, that I cheated on my LSAT exam, and that I was a convicted shoplifter. Turns out that it was Stan who slept with all of his female college professors just so he could get himself into a good law school, that his son was a convicted shoplifter, and that his wife was the one who cheated on her LSAT exam, but never could be found guilty of it. Wow!

Doug kissed me then. He put my hands into his. Doug squeezed my hands. Doug said that he wanted to be with me and only me and that he planned to make it up to me for the rest of his life.

We are so happy after being married for a year. I am now 8 months pregnant with twins. Life could not get any better than this and I could not have asked for more. I really hope that my life stays this way for good.